SMALL REGRETS

Donated to
Augustana University College
by

William C. Latta

SMALL REGRETS
DAVE MARGOSHES

THISTLEDOWN PRESS

Canadian Cataloguing in Publication Data

Margoshes, Dave, 1941-
Small regrets

ISBN 0-920633-18-8 (bound).
ISBN 0-920633-19-6 (pbk).

I. Title.
PS8576.A734S5 1986 C813'.54 C86-098033-2
PR9199.3.M57S5 1986

Book design by A.M. Forrie
Cover painting by Stephen McDonnell

Typesetting by Pièce de Résistance, Edmonton
Set in 11 point Plantin

Printed and bound in Canada by
Hignell Printing Limited, Winnipeg

Thistledown Press Ltd.
668 East Place
Saskatoon, Sask.
S7J 2Z5

Acknowledgements

"One Too Many Mornings", "Trespassers Will Be Violated", "The Caller", "Mister
Maestro", and "Rabbit Done Run etc." previously appeared in *Descant*; "The Same
Thing" and "Truckee Your Blues Away" in *Dalhousie Review*; "A False Moustache"
in *Prism international*; "A Change of Life" in *Malahat Review*; "Among Strangers"
in *WRIT*; "On an April Morning" in *Quixote*. "A Change of Life", "Truckee Your
Blues Away" and "Rabbit Done Run etc." also appeared in *Third Impressions*
(Oberon, 1982), and "Mister Maestro" appeared in *Best Canadian Stories 1986*
(Oberon).

The author would like to acknowledge the assistance of the Alberta Culture Film
and Literary Arts Branch in preparing this collection.

This book has been published with the assistance of the Saskatchewan Arts Board
and the Canada Council.

FOR ILYA

and with thanks to John Metcalf

CONTENTS

THE SAME THING

The man in the pink bathrobe went directly up to the girl who was sunning herself on the beach. She was slim and muscular, a tennis player, deeply tanned, with blond hair that rolled off her head in all directions like a lion's mane.

"Excuse me, may I speak to you?" he asked. He had a deep, hushed voice like her father used in the library when men came to visit, and he was about her father's age. His eyes, though, were startlingly blue; she couldn't recall the color of her father's eyes.

"Of course, what a silly thing to say." She raised her head, blinking into the sun.

"This will sound like a sillier thing," he said. He squatted down beside her and looked directly into her face. She was very pretty because she was young. She looked seventeen but probably was nineteen, he thought. In fact, she was twenty. In a few years, she would be an attractive woman and a man in love with her would call her lovely, but she wouldn't really be that. Her nose was a bit too big, her jaw too slack.

"I'd like to, uh, have sex with you."

The girl laughed, very cleanly, clearly, with real amusement, as if someone had said something funny.

"I didn't mean it to be funny," the man said. "I'm very serious."

He sounded serious, the girl thought. She looked at him more closely, wondering if she should be frightened. There were people on the beach within shouting distance, so she decided not to be. He was a nice looking man, with a face like a shoe, worn and comfortable, and sandy hair that was in need of cutting. He wore black-framed glasses that made him look like a college professor or a bank clerk. Behind the thin lenses, the blue eyes were clear and unblinking.

"Well, I'm very flattered," she said, looking away. "That's very nice to hear."

The man smiled. "I see. I didn't intend the remark merely as a compliment. I would really like to." He looked away briefly, as if out of shyness.

The girl forced a smile. It didn't seem funny anymore. "I don't sleep with strangers," she said. She tried not to sound hostile.

"Sleep," he said. "That's such a strange way of putting it. At any rate, of course not. I didn't expect that you did. This is different, however. I'll pay you."

"I'm not a prostitute," the girl said sharply.

"Of course not. I didn't mean to imply that I thought you were." He smiled now, openly and warmly, as if the difficult part were over. "But everyone"—he paused, and sighed deeply—"has their price, as they say."

The girl made a face and lowered her head for a moment. When she raised it, she realized the man was gazing over her head at her backside. She felt naked suddenly. "I don't think I have a price," she said slowly.

"I see, of course." He made a little laugh, then straightened his face. "Would five thousand be enough?"

"Five thousand? Dollars?"

"Of course."

"Excuse me, mister." The girl got up and began to gather in her towel, sunglasses and book. It was a paperback *Gatsby*.

"Don't go. I'm not crazy, nor am I kidding. I'm quite serious." He told her his name. "Does that mean anything to you?"

She regarded him with her head cocked to the side, studying his worn face, brushing absently at flecks of sand on the bottom of her bikini. "Oil or railroads or something," she said finally.

"Yes. Or something. Many somethings." He stood up and pushed his face closer to hers. "I'm sure you've seen this in the paper. I don't mean that to be boastful, but it does get in quite often."

"Last week," the girl said hesitantly.

"Yes, yes, last week." He seemed tired of the game she was forcing him to play. He looked at her admiringly. Her legs were long and supple. Her breasts were small but well shaped, like spring avocados, and they didn't sag. Her mouth, in relation to her nose, was too small, and he noticed for the first time the remarkable evenness of her teeth. As a girl, she had worn braces for years.

"The money means nothing to me," he said. "Absolutely nothing. I make that much or more in an hour, any hour, so spending that sum in an hour means nothing."

"You can write it off as a business expense," the girl said with some bitterness. She had had an argument about that with her father once.

"Yes, yes," he waved his hand impatiently. "I don't bother with such things. What do you say?"

The girl hesitated. She was thinking hard.

"Why me?"

"I like your looks."

"Do you usually do it this way? I mean, just go up to a girl and..." her voice trailed off.

"Yes. Sometimes one of my assistants makes the arrangements, sometimes I do it myself if I'm alone. Let me be clear. I am very rich. I can have anything I want. I don't like to deprive myself. I like your looks. I want to have sex with you. What could be simpler?" He looked away, out to sea. A boy on a surfboard was coming crashing in, tumbling like an eel. Above him, a white gull reeled like the hand of an orchestra conductor. "And, yes, of course, I will pay you five thousand dollars. Isn't that enough?"

"Yes," the girl said quetly.

"It will take a very short time," the man said, brightening. He smiled, pointing up the slope. "I've rented the villa there, just over the ridge. Can you come there now?"

"I suppose," the girl said.

"It won't be as unpleasant as you think," he said. "I won't paw you or slaver over you. I'll make no demands of you, actually, or make any attempt to satisfy you, for that matter. I just want to watch you, look at your body, then use it." He looked away. "Very quickly."

They walked across the sand and the girl felt cold. "Do you mind if we talk?" she asked.

"Of course not." His blue eyes peered at her intently through his glasses. "This isn't something so horrible, I'm not a monster." He stopped. "You don't think of me as a monster, do you?"

The girl shivered, trying to hold her shoulders steady. She saw that he saw them shake. "No." Then: "Brrr, it's getting kind of chilly."

"We'll be there in a minute." They walked on.

"You do this often?" the girl asked.

The man shrugged. "Now and then. No, more than that, I suppose. Yes. Once a week, something like that."

The girl whistled.

He smiled. "It's not as extraordinary as you think. How often do you have a Coke, or a Pepsi?"

"You mean me?"

"Yes, of course."

"I don't know, once a day, maybe twice. Some days not at all."

"Whenever you feel like it, in other words."

"I guess so."

"And how much does it cost you?"

"A quarter, thirty cents, something like that."

"I see. You can afford to spend a quarter or two a day, I suppose."

The girl laughed. "Not always. But, yeah, I suppose I can."

"Yes. And do you really need to buy a Coke? Couldn't you just as well drink water?"

"I see what you mean," the girl said. People were different from soft drinks, weren't they?

"I know what you're thinking," the man said. "It's not the same thing. But it is, my dear. Think about it some more. It is the same thing."

They came to the house and went in. It was a long, L-shaped house that she knew, had passed by often on the beach. It was on a ridge, apart from the other beach houses, and it looked out at the sea from a height that made the horizon stretch just a little bit farther than it appeared from the beach. She could see fluttering white sails in the distance, like folded handkerchiefs floating above the water.

"What's your name?" the man asked. He took off the pink bathrobe. He was wearing tan beach shorts, knee-length, and a white web tee shirt. His arms were pale, hairless.

"Charlotte."

"Charlotte. That's an old-fashioned sort of name." He smiled, so as not to offend her. "You don't hear it very often. It's nice."

"It's after some movie star," Charlotte said. "From the forties."

"I see. Would you like a drink?" He went to the bar at the far end of the livingroom, near the picture window. "I'm going to have something."

"No, thank you," Charlotte said.

"A Coke? Pepsi?" He smiled and she thought he must be mocking her.

"I don't want one just now," she said icily, thinking she was proving something. But then she thought: no, that's just restraint, it doesn't mean you want to do without. Or can.

"Well, I'm having something," he said. He clinked bottles. "I'll just be a minute or two."

"Take your time," the girl said. She wandered around the large room, stared into the unlit fireplace, gazed at a Matisse on the white, finely textured wall. She had thought, as they approached the house, that if he was a fake he would show it then, would grab her, try to rape her in the bushes growing densely out of the sand, but she would be too quick for him, would slip out of his hands, run, shrieking, exhilarated. But now they were inside. He had opened the door with a key.

"Are you really Stanley?" she asked abruptly.

He looked up from his glass, his worn face perplexed. "Would you like to see my ID? Like at a bar? You must be asked for proof of age often enough. You are over 18, aren't you?"

"Yes."

"And not a virgin, I trust."

"No. Would you have preferred I were?"

"Not especially. No, not at all."

"I thought men liked virgins, that it turned them on to be the first."

He observed her in silence for a moment, sipping from a highball glass. "Some men do, perhaps. Personally, I find it too much of a chore. The conversation is about to become vulgar, don't you think?"

Charlotte laughed. "Are you prudish?"

His face darkened for a second. "Not prudish, no, but I don't like to be vulgar."

"I'm sorry." She sat down on the edge of a long white sofa. "But you *are* Stanley?"

The man sighed. "Yes." He went through a door into another room without another word. The girl wondered if she was supposed to follow, but she waited. The air conditioning wasn't on and it was hot in the house. She was sorry she had refused a drink. She was thinking of going to the bar and finding something for herself when he came back and handed her a magazine, folded open. His picture was on the page, the blue eyes glittering through glasses at the camera with interest. She read a few paragraphs.

"Very impressive."

"It's only money." He shrugged. "That's a cliché, I know, but it happens to be true. It's pieces of paper you fold and put in your pocket and people will cut your throat to get it so they can put it in *their* pockets. By itself, it doesn't mean a thing."

"Then why do you pursue it?" Charlotte asked.

He smiled, blowing air through his nose. "Why do you drink a Coke when you're thirsty?"

"It's the same thing? Now you are stretching," she said. She took a cigarette from a silver tray on the marble coffee table and lit it with a gold lighter shaped like a teardrop.

"Perhaps. At any rate, I hope you're satisfied that I am who I said I am." He took the magazine from her, closed it and tossed it onto the sofa lightly. "And that I'm not going to murder you or rape you. And that I can afford to buy a few moments of your time."

"My time," Charlotte said bitterly.

"I see. All right, your body. Your cunt, do you prefer that? I'm buying your cunt so I can stick my cock into it and come in it. Is that vulgar enough?" His face was dark and his voice had a sharp edge to it, like ruffled sheets of paper.

"I'm sorry," Charlotte said. She lowered her head, studying her bare feet. There was sand between her toes and she leaned down and flicked some of the grains onto the deep blue rug. She could hear the clinking of ice as he finished his drink. She still had time to change her mind, she thought.

"I didn't mean to raise my voice," the man said presently.

"That's all right. I'm sorry I was...vulgar." She swallowed.

"Shall we get on with it?" He took off his shirt, pulling it over his head. His chest was spindly, with a cleft in the middle and reddish hairs around the nipples.

The girl felt, suddenly, nauseous. "I could blackmail you, couldn't I? Has that ever happened?"

The man looked at her coldly, his lips squeezed together as if he were kissing the air. He was still holding the shirt in his hands. He walked stiffly to the hallway and opened the door.

"Good day, young lady. I'm sorry we were not able to conduct ourselves more reasonably."

"I didn't say I was going to blackmail you," Charlotte called after him. She didn't get up. "I was just asking."

He stood rigidly beside the open door, glaring at her.

"I wouldn't do a thing like that." She made her voice sound as if she was hurt.

"I didn't expect you would." The man closed the door softly and came back into the livingroom. "It would be foolish to try such a thing. But I don't like you even thinking of it. I'm not a pathetic weakling who can be twisted around the finger of a woman. I'm not a pervert. I'm not sick." His voice didn't rise but he was clearly angry. "There isn't really anything you could blackmail me over. That I had sex with you? So what. That I paid you for it? So what. But I don't like the implication. I don't like what you're thinking. It isn't true. I'm only buying something I happen to want, with money that I can easily afford to spend, and no one is being hurt by it. You only think it's odd because you could never afford to do the same thing, except that you do, of course, all the time, in different ways." He paused, the anger expelled, and smiled wanly. "By the way, what will you do with the money?"

"Go away," Charlotte said.

"Just that?"

"Just that."

"I see." He looked down at his hands, folded the shirt neatly in half and laid it on the sofa next to the magazine. "Perhaps you should get ready."

The girl stood up. She looked very pretty, clean, straight, sexy. Her skin had a soft, healthy glow. The tiny hairs covering her skin like a fur of gauze were brown from the sun, almost gold. "I'm ready," she said.

"The bathroom is through the hall," the man said, raising his chin.

The girl looked at him stupidly.

"Hadn't you better do something?"

"I don't know what you mean."

He hesitated, reluctant to speak. "I appreciate that I'm not exciting to you. Hadn't you better..." —he paused, looking away through the window at the sea and the shimmering blue sky— "manipulate yourself, do something to make yourself open and... wet." He stumbled over the last word. "I don't want to hurt you. Or myself." He smiled apologetically. "This is supposed to be pleasurable for me."

"Of course," the girl said.

"There's a jar of Vaseline in the bathroom," the man said. "If you want it."

She went through the hallway to the bathroom. She was sick.

"Please come back with your bathing suit still on," the man called from the hallway.

He had drawn the drapes and turned on the lights. The living-room seemed different now, smaller, airless. He was lighting the fire, adjusting the gas tap. "I thought you might still be chilly." He smiled up at her, trying to make her feel more comfortable. He could see how tense she was.

The girl shivered. She felt hot and cold at the same time. The Vaseline felt clammy on her thighs.

"In here?" she asked.

"Yes, on the rug."

"Wouldn't the bed be more comfortable?"

"For you, perhaps," he said shortly. "I prefer the rug. You won't be on it long enough for it to matter."

The girl stood in the middle of the room, her mouth dry. The man had taken off his shorts and was naked. He sat down on the sofa, so that she was standing between him and the fire. His penis hung limply against his thigh, lifeless, larger than she would have thought. She knew that made no difference. She tried to avert her eyes but found she couldn't.

"Take off your top," he said. "Slowly."

She started toward him.

"No, stay there. Stay where you are."

The girl stared at him. She hooked her arms behind her and undid the catch. She tried to remember the way the girl at that bar on the boardwalk did it. She brought her right hand up to her breasts and took hold of the bra, then brought up her left hand. She cupped her breasts. The man's penis jerked and began to crawl along his thigh, thickening. She watched it in fascination, trying not to think. She dropped her hands.

"Turn around," the man said. His voice had thickened slightly. "Take off your bottom. Don't unhook it, just slide it down. Slowly."

The girl put her hands on her hips and slid the cloth down.

"Stop."

She could hear his breathing.

"Let them drop down now."

She gave the panties a little push, then let them slide down her legs. She felt, suddenly, ashamed.

"Put your hand in front of you, there, and turn around," the man said. "Slowly."

She turned, stepping out of the panties. She closed her eyes.

"That's all right," he said. "you don't have to look."

The girl swallowed hard. She felt the warmth of the fire on her buttocks and she took a small step backwards.

"Move your hand away," the man said. "Spread your legs a little." His breath was loud, rasping, like he had a cold. "You can lie down now."

Charlotte turned her back so she wouldn't have to see him and lay down on the rug. It was deep and soft, like the sea.

"Don't look so terrified," the man said. "You've done this before. It's the same. Spread your arms and your legs. Raise your knees." She could hear him get up from the sofa and come toward her. Her head was close to the fire and her hair felt warm. "And smile, for God's sake. That's the least you can do."

"The least," she said. She had to clench her teeth to keep them from chattering.

"Yes," the man said. He crawled between her legs, touched her once with a finger and entered her. "Oh, God," he said.

There were tears in the girl's eyes. Over his shoulder, she could see the drapes covering the picture window. She imagined they were open and she was gazing at a clear blue sky. There were whitecaps on the water and gulls chasing each other across the sun, blocking out the light. She felt the first slide, then she felt nothing. She knew he was moving above her, but she didn't feel him. She felt nothing. The gulls were cawing, scolding her for disturbing them. Their wings were white on the inside but there were streaks of grey on the ouside. There was one that had a grey blotch on its chest, like a stain where an animal had done something dirty in the snow. The man made a noise like a hurt bird and fell heavily against her. "God," he said again. After a moment, he rolled away from her.

The girl got up and put on her bathing suit.

"Would you like a drink now?" the man asked. He was still

lying on the rug, flat on his back, one knee raised, his face glowing from the fire. "A Pepsi?" There was contempt in his voice.

"No. I'd like to go now."

"I see." After a moment, the man got up. "I'll get you your money."

"Please put on your clothes," Charlotte said.

He went out of the room. When he came back he had on a bathrobe, different from the one he'd worn on the beach. He handed her an envelope. "I think you'd have trouble cashing a cheque so large. I hope you don't mind carrying so much cash."

The girl opened the envelope. "I've never seen so much money," she said.

The man shook his head. "It's real, I assure you. And it's all there, but you can count it if you desire."

The girl closed the envelope and held it tightly in her fist. "Was it good for you?" she asked him coldly. "Did you enjoy yourself?" She wanted to hurt him, to make him feel small. She wanted to make him feel as loathsome as she herself did.

He shrugged. "It was all right," he said lamely.

Charlotte looked at him sharply. "Is that all? All right?" She thought that, later, she could come back with a gun and kill him. Or she and a friend, a boy she knew, could hold him and hurt him until he gave them money, lots of it, it meant so little to him. Or she could set this house on fire during the night, while he slept.

He shrugged again. "It was wonderful. Best ever. You are one great fuck. Feel better?"

"That's very funny," the girl said. "You're a real comedian."

"I thought you were in a hurry to go."

Charlotte picked up her book and her sunglasses. She looked around for her towel. There wasn't any way, she realized suddenly, that she could hurt him as much as she already had. She went to the door and opened it, blinking her eyes in the bright sunlight. She squeezed the envelope, feeling the thick wad of bills. She turned around. He was sitting on the sofa smoking a cigarette, watching her. Behind the lenses of his glasses, his blue eyes were flat as the sky.

"Would you like me to come again?" she asked abruptly. She held up the envelope.

The man in the bathrobe snorted through his nose, smiling crookedly. "No, thank you."

The girl continued to stand there, looking at him. "I wasn't that bad," she said.

"You were fine," the man said, sighing. He got up and opened the drapes, standing in the centre of the window so that he blocked out a good deal of the sun. "I hate to be crude."

"Go ahead," Charlotte said.

The man shook his head slowly, as if he were explaining to a child why he should not stick his fingers in the fire. "You've been used," he said. He thought for a moment, then added: "Flat."

ONE TOO MANY MORNINGS

It was a fine day. A bank of clouds was fingerpainted across the sky above the stand of poplars. The scent of hemp and corn wafted down the valley and the leaves of grass in their meadow rubbed against each other sensually, singing.

Crit lay spreadeagled, his limbs pinned to weeds by bands of sun. A deep compress of blue pressed down on the ridge of forehead and brow above his eyes and pinpricks of heat danced madly along the arc of his ears. Insects, startled but adventurous, foraged through his scalp and were crushed as he twitched; some lucky ones took refuge beneath his cowlick and were spared.

Beside him, Rachel spread her legs and took his hand to shield her. The touch set his bonds free and he sat up, startled, but lazily, rolling over onto the crooked brace of one arm, lifting his dizzied head against the weight of day. Beneath his gaze, she shimmered, the tips of her skin in hushed motion. Seas of hair like mist swept over, tickling his eyes. If I took the time, he thought, to count each one, I'd go blind before I'd half be done.

"Do you remember," he said, "when we were children and I hated you, for no better reason than that you were a girl, *different* from me, and I pulled your pigtails in the schoolyard? And then later, in the fourth grade, or was it the fifth, we went into the cloakroom and I said if you show me yours I'll show you mine, and you pulled up your skirt and your pants down and I looked at it but then I ran away without showing you mine and you were so mad? And then at the prom I danced with you and took you outside in the moonlight and copped a feel? You had tissue paper there and I pulled it out but underneath it was soft and warm and I said I could feel them growing and you put your hand on me and said you could feel it growing too and we laughed. And then in high school we went into the hayloft that evening of Hallowe'en while all the others were driving around having egg and tomato fights, and I was so fumbly and we got hay in our asses and almost fell out of the loft? And then all those times that summer when we'd go skinny-dipping in the creek at night and your skin would glisten in the star drips and we tried to do it in the water and almost drowned? Do you remember all those times, those moments when our love was new and innocent, that happy time before I went away to the war and your letters began to become distant and vague, and then dwindled off into just Christmas cards once a month and then into nothing? Until I came back to find you? Until I came back to the land which spawned both you and I and our burning love, back to try, desperately, to recapture that...that...whatever it was? Do you remember?''

''No,'' Rachel said. While he was talking she had taken a cigarette from the pack in his shirt, which lay crumpled within reach, lighted it, inhaled deeply and blown smoke rings. Now she studied the glowing ash, as if searching for something there. ''Was there really such a thing? Did you do horrendous things like that to some poor girl? Who was she? What did she taste like? Was she as slippery as I? Had she acne?''

''Yes, she did,'' Crit said. He rolled over onto his back and lay at attention, his spine straight beneath him, his head lifted gently by the protestation of weary grass. He returned his hand to its perch on her and observed his erection towering lean and unconcerned between the tips of his toes. ''Yes, she had acne. She was as slippery as an afterbirth. She tasted like socks. She was the girl with her hair in an inkwell, another in a closet, still another with a corsage and tissue padding, yet another with hay in her ass. And a dream in star drips. Such, in a nut, is my sexual history, my heritage. And what," he rolled again to his side to ease a tickling along his spine and observed the impossible horizon the deeps and shallows of her made, "was yours?"

Rachel was silent. Streams of smoke drifted from her mouth like steam rising from a fissure in the earth. She said nothing.

"Methinks the lady doth protest too little," Crit said. "Methinks the lady has a past as sordid as the gentleman's. But, then, aren't things supposed to be that way? Surely you don't mean to tell me that I myself *actually* invented the sins and weaknesses which I have always claimed as my own? *Do you mean to tell me?*" He took the cigarette gently from her lips, puffed on it once, as if to determine for himself its existence, and crushed the living end of it in his fingers. "That I was alone?"

"I mean to tell you," Rachel said, arching her shoulders, "that I have grass in my ass."

"I'll brush it off," Crit said, and sat up, slid himself in front of her, raised her knees. Instead, he ate it off. Green slices of juice stained his cheeks and later *she* wiped them off, with her tongue.

Suffering shuddered to a halt then. Whatever there had been diffused itself in the air about them; all that had been lacking became. The first slippery resistance faded and blended into the long slide of sweet friction that ends too suddenly, too swiftly, in the beginning of still another ascending. Then movement which seemed apart from them, distant. Far beyond the poplars, Crit could see, between swaying branches, cattle grazing, a lone horseman, a sea of turkeys swelling up like a tide behind a barefoot boy who led them on with promises, a windmill lazy in the breeze. He could see it turning, the blades rising and falling with a pulse slower than breathing. He counted the swings and with each turn he rose, slowly, with each turn he fell.

His elbows and his knees dug into the dirt beneath the grass and his toes flexed each time his body moved, and her breasts pressed up against his chest and her hair swayed along his throat and face and sweat welled under his arms and along his thighs. Her face gleamed below him, the fine hair of her cheeks lank and soft against the taut skin, and lines careered from her mouth where he hadn't known them before, twisted to a silent yes and yes and yes again, to her nostrils, pear-shaped, breathing steam toward his eyes. There was a smudge of dirt on her cheek, just below her eye where amber flecks danced in the green like dolphins in the sea. On her skin there were gentle pores, thousands of them, my god, some but slopes, others canyons, still others craters of the moon. He hated himself for thinking about it that way. If I took the time, he thought, to count each one, I'd go blind...

The sweet smell of her pierced him, setting the hairs in his nostrils on edge, bringing the taste of crushed grapes to the root of his tongue.

Afterwards, tinkling bells could be heard in the distance, as if through water. A mother lion crept cautiously past them, gave a sly, curious glance in their direction, and called for her cub: if you're late you'll miss your dinner.

All the clouds were gone and the sky had become transparent; God's smiling face could be seen clearly beyond, his jowls working furiously as he chewed at the something which offered resistance, the clouds perhaps. The stand of poplars had scattered; some sat, gazing blankly at them, others knelt, as if saying prayers. And the bugs were gone; they'd fled from the tremor of the earthquake.

"As if," Crit said aloud, "I've rid Ireland of insects. I'll be a saint."

From her side there was nothing. She was not asleep—far from it—but her eyes were closed, one lid quivering faintly. A lash, disengaged, hovered precariously close to her nose. Inside her, Crit thought, all is serene while, outside, lions prowl. It's dangerous. A man could get eaten. Why do I quit her? Why do I always emerge again and again, like an ostrich peering up from the sand to see if the elephants have gone by? One could lose one's head quite easily.

"Do shut up," Rachel said.

Her nostrils were like walnuts, and Crit hated her suddenly, but was afraid to say so, even to himself. Why had he brought her here, he wondered—here, to his places, if only for this? If she goes, he thought, well, she goes.

He rose, wiping grass from his legs and arms, and stretched achingly, holding his outflung pose until he grew dizzy from counting the fingers of his right hand—through his right eye, the other one closed, the windmill in the distance was framed between his thumb and first finger; through his left eye, the windmill was all but obscured by the thumb, and with both eyes open there were two windmills and way too many fingers.

"Get up," he said. "I'll give you the finger, I'll give you all my extra fingers. Get up." He waved one finger, one he felt he could spare, in her face, like a baton, hoping for the swelling of music.

"Thank you, but no, thank you," she said, sitting up, opening her mouth as if to bite his finger, snapping at air. "I'm quite satisfied as it is. Rub my back."

"No, get up," he said, but he came around behind her, knelt in the grass and touched her back softly with his fingertips. There were reddish marks on her skin, and the impression of blades of grass, as the image of the Queen is often left to ponder which direction to head on a railroad track after its penny has been powdered by a freight. He could see quite clearly the veins of the grass clinging stubbornly above the translucent veins which spidered their way under her fragile skin.

He slapped her lightly on the back of the neck. "Get up, really, now. Put your clothes on."

Rachel wobbled on her haunches, muttering under her breath, then catapulted to her feet and stumbled forward, arched herself against the horizon. The sun, on the decline, was obscured for a moment by her head, sending a barrage of fragmented rays into Crit's eyes. "You bastard," she said.

Their clothes were scattered all about and it took several minutes of intense hunting to find them all. Crit dressed quickly, not bothering to button his shirt nor tie the laces of his moccasins, sat himself on the stump of a tree and watched her. She dressed slowly, as if doing a striptease in reverse. She took particular care with each snap and button and fussed for some time with the folded cuffs on the sleeves of her blouse. She had trouble closing the zipper on her jeans. "You're getting fat," Crit said.

He got up from the stump and let her sit to tie the laces of her tennis shoes, and he stood beside her, staring at the sun, running his fingers through her hair. When she was finished, she planted both feet firmly on the ground in front of her but sat immobily, her head bent down, her eyes boring a groove through the grass and top soil and shale beneath, down through the crust of the earth. Way, far, far away, Crit fancied, she must be seeing Chinamen walking on the soles of their feet, their toes gently curling toward her.

"You *are* a bastard," she said, finally, at the moment that the sun became entangled in the witches hair smothering the tops of the poplars in the distance. A chill sprang up around them, as if the grass, holding its breath since morning, had at last exhaled.

Crit sighed too, and watched his breath struggle through the air until it succumbed to the diffusion hovering there before him, just out of reach, smiling as it waited. It was a far distance from here to where he was a moment before, a further distance yet to where he was now, and no one would ever span the distance between here and where he would go.

"If you show me yours," he said, affecting a smile, "I'll show you mine."

A FALSE MOUSTACHE

In 1925, when my father came back to New York from Cleveland, he moved uptown to Harlem, where he hoped to find independence.

He was seven years older than the century, still a young man, and had spent three years on a small Yiddish newspaper learning the craft he would earn his living by for the next forty. His father and brother were both well-known journalists and it had been important for him to make his own name, on his own, and he'd gone so far, in Cleveland, as to actually change his name, to Morgenstern, which means morning star. He liked to tell me, years later, that he would often dream, in the cold rooming house attic he'd shared with a mouse he called Maleka, of returning to the city he'd once thought didn't have room for him, the city of his father's and brother's friends and influence, their reputation, like a bright morning star, burning on the horizon, forcing men to lift their heads and see.

In those days, with the war still seeming to reverberate in the air above the city like a subway train that has rumbled out of sight but not hearing, Harlem was already beginning to make the change which was to plunge it into the new world. The handsome brownstones which lined 125th Street and its dissecting avenues were starting the painful process of transforming themselves into neat, genteel boarding houses, like capped teeth in a once proud mouth—the smile is still warm, but it no longer glitters. My father took a room on the second floor of a Lexington Avenue house that had once belonged to a lawyer with Tammany connections. The lawyer had died in debt and now his solemn parlor was the domain of an aunt who had only her wits and boarders to keep her together. The room was clean, with a scrubbed window behind starched white curtains looking out on the avenue and one slim slice of Grammercy Park, one block south, that wasn't cut off by the buildings across the way. North of 125th, where the roots were deeper or the money of better quality, my father didn't know which, there were still families with servants living in the pillared, imposing brownstones, and from his window, on warm afternoons, he could watch the black nursemaids, who lived far south of the pleasant street, strolling with their charges to the park, where they would sit on benches and watch the children play in the sun. He paid twelve dollars a week, and that included coffee and rolls in the morning, dinner sharply at six. When he worked the night shift, as he often did, his landlady packed him a wholesome lunch.

There was no mouse in the room on Lexington Avenue and, even though the subway ride downtown to Lower Broadway took almost an hour, my father enjoyed living there, far from the sights and smells that meant something different entirely. And his enjoyment was enhanced somewhat when, after several weeks, he ran into Shmelke in the hall outside his room.

"Shmelke," my father said, surprised and pleased, still new enough in his surroundings to be lonely, "what brings you here?"

"I have to go," Shmelke shrugged, gesturing toward the toilet at the end of the hall. At the other end, my father could see, a door hung open, the door to the room where, he believed, a traveling salesman with a lingerie firm resided. Or had.

"So go," my father said, moving out of the lean man's way, "but step in on your way back and begin the process again."

A minute later, they were lifting their water glasses to the memory of Cleveland. "May that infernal lake from which blows that infernal cold wind overspill its shores and swallow the infernal

city up,'' Shmelke said, licking his lips with a peculiar slap-
ping sound, like small waves on stones. He swallowed the
whiskey with a single gulp.

He was a tall, fleshless man with ears like mushrooms springing out of moist earth, fond of suits a size too large, as if he
expected to suddenly put on weight. His lips were the size and
color of the patches on a worn inner tube. He was altogether
the most homely man my father had ever known, quite an
accomplishment in a world populated by men who worked too
hard or kept their heads on too lofty planes to be physically vain.

"It was my partner, that infermal rascal Goldblatt, who forced
me to descend,'' Shmelke said in explanation for his presence,
both in the city and these modest surroundings. He was a
humorless, literal man whose command of his second language
was not up to his reach.

"The ticket selling?'' my father inquired after a moment's
thought. They had not been friends, by any means, but they
had frequented the same cafe in Cleveland, a sort of expatriate
Cafe Royale filled with poets, newspapermen, actors, artists,
musicians and hangers-on, and during the three years he had
known of half a dozen different ventures in which Shmelke had
been involved. Artists' representative was what he liked to call
himself; press agent was closer to the truth; ticket agent was,
in fact, what he was the last time my father had heard.

"Let me tell you, that was no sofa on roses, that expedition.
It was a service, a struggle of love, something to do for the people, you know what I mean, Morgenstern? You think I could
make a dollar on a thing like that?''

"Would I argue with you?'' my father asked. He poured
another two fingers of whiskey into the dusty glasses.

"My partner, what a *shlimazal*, a head for business he had
on his shoulders as big as this.'' Shmelke held up his thumb,
examined it critically then replaced it with his pinky. "As big
as this, no bigger.'' He gulped down the whiskey with a rubbery slap. "We had these tickets, this big order, something really
expressive, for opera, Caruso, no, not him, but someone just
as infamous, and it brought in a lot of money. A lot? It made

me enervated having that much money so close. And was I right?''
He slapped his narrow forehead with the palm of his hand. ''That
infernal *shmegega* had a chance—a *chance*, he called it, a hole in
the ground would be more like it—to buy up a whole theatre for
Gilbert and Sullivan, so he used all the money from the opera
tickets. The whole cat and caboodle.''

''Sounds like a smart move,'' my father said naively.

''A smart move? Sure, like suicide is smart for the widow and
the dolphins.'' Shmelke glared at my father as if he were in the
company of a fool. My father tipped the bottle over the glasses.

''So there comes the man from the opera saying where's the
money from the tickets? So what do we say?''

''Tomorrow?'' my father offered.

Shmelke peered at him with skeptical admiration. ''Sure, tomorrow, that's context. But what happens after tomorrow?''

''Gilbert and Sullivan is sold?''

''Morgenstern, no offensive, but you and my infernal partner
Goldblatt would be sweethearts, regular darlings, newlyweds you
could be.''

''You couldn't sell Gilbert and Sullivan?''

Shmelke's watery eyes rolled up and almost disappeared into
his eyelids. ''Morgenstern, you can *always* sell Gilbert and Sullivan.
In Cleveland, Gilbert could be elected mayor, Sullivan the mayor,
maybe.''

''So what's the problem?''

''Problem? Who said anything about a problem? Morgenstern,
you surprise me. *Problem?* What a cryptic. No problem, believe
me. The Gilbert and Sullivan money goes to the opera and that
accounting is closed, the book is finished, *kaput*. A little incon-
sideration, maybe, when the Gilbert and Sullivan cancels and
there's the refunds to make, but a *problem? Noooo.*''

Shmelke glared at my father, challenging him, and, though he
was tempted to say he didn't understand, my father held his
tongue. After that, the two men saw each other often, in the
hallway outside the toilet, rather than at the dinner table, as my
father was then working nights, and often they would share a glass
of whiskey in my father's room, occasionally in Shmelke's. The

man did not bathe often and there was an odor in his room which
my father found worth the price of his whiskey to avoid.

It was spring when my father moved into the room in Harlem
and the city was opening itself up for him the way leaves and
blossoms open themselves up to the insects that float on the
warm breezes of April and May. The Jewish life of New York
was rich and exciting in those days, its theatre vigorous, its
literature strong and searching, its artists bold and sensitive with
a freedom growing out of a new sense of purpose after a hundred
years or more of lying low. There were a half a dozen Yiddish
dailies in the city then and the competition between them was
fierce, their pages filled with essays on the arts and philosophy,
criticism, Talmudic debate, humor, advice on everything from
self-improvement to affairs of the heart and body, along with
news of the far-flung community and the world at large that
owed as much, in its style and presentation, to Hearst and
Pulitzer as it did to Spinoza and the learned rabbis of Poland
and Russia. My father was a news writer, not an essayist, toil-
ing for the paper called *Der Tag*, or The Day, but he loved the
company of the great men he drank coffee with in the cafeteria
at the corner of East Broadway and Delancy Street and at the
Cafe Royale, where the lights burned all through the night like
beacons.

Sometimes, he would encounter Shmelke there. The tall,
skinny man with the pennant ears had secured a position as press
agent to a rabbinical council and was also doing publicity work
for a hospital in the Bronx. But his heart and soul belonged
to the arts and he often could be found in the evenings at the
Cafe Royale and other warm, bright rooms that sparkled through
the gray streets of the lower east side like fireflies.

"Morgenstern, Morgenstern, join us. Sit down, my friend.
Combine with me a drink. You know Rubenstein and Pashka?"

"Of course." My father sat, smiling. Despite the invitation,
he knew he would pay for the whiskey he ordered.

"Rubenstein, the steamed violinist, and Pashka, the clammed
dramatist. Morgenstern, the novelist and poet."

My father knew both men—one a teacher of music at a

Hebrew school, the other a stage hand at the theatre across the street—and the conversation was good, the evening warm. He lingered, although it was late. Shmelke and he rode home together on the subway.

"Come in, have a drink," Shmelke begged. "I've got something to show you."

My father's curiosity was stronger than his tiredness and he followed the bobbing head with its ballast ears into the cluttered room, rich with the smell of socks. On the rumpled bed, there was a peaked white cap like those he had seen the black nursemaids in the park wearing. Shmelke snatched it up and twirled it on a finger, grinning darkly.

There was a bottle of cheap rye on the dresser and my father poured two glasses.

"You should see her, Morgenstern," Shmelke said. "An angel, a dark angel, like devilsfood cake, like an animal of the night."

My father was moved by the intensity and clarity of Shmelke's description. He swallowed his drink and took out a cigarette. "You've had this woman here? In your room?"

"Right *here*," Shmelke grinned, patting the twisted bedclothes. "Why not?" He tossed the cap carelessly onto the bed, shrugging his shoulders. "What do I care what people think?"

"Very commendable, my friend, but does that include our landlady?"

The rubbery lips smacked at the rim of his glass. "Depression, depression, Morgenstern, is the soul of valor." He winked.

"And the girl? She's nice?"

Shmelke laughed, a cackling that reminded my father of the chickens that used to share the kitchen of his mother's farmhouse in the winter, years before, when he'd been a boy. "Nice, what's nice? To the Cafe Royale, I don't intend to bring her. *Here*, she's nice." He pointed to the bed.

"Is it wise, though, one of those girls?" my father asked cautiously.

"Morgenstern, of you I'm shameless." Shmelke fixed him with a stern gaze, the rims of his elephant ears reddening slightly. "A man like you, a spigot."

During that first year of his return to the city, when my father was firmly establishing himself as a newspaperman, and some time before he would meet my mother, he had love affairs of his own, great friendships, nights of talk and whiskey and coffee that lasted till dawn. He was active in the Jewish Writers Guild, which got its start at the same time as the Newspaper Guild but soon outstripped its English language rival. He got a raise. And one night, in late summer, he was witness to a murder and wrote a story that made an impression on his editors.

My father had an interest in labor, but there already was a labor editor on the paper, a stern old man who had been a scholar and teacher in the old country and who wrote with the grace of an albatross. When this man, Jaffe, was busy, my father was often pressed into service to help him if there was a conflict, and on an evening in September he went to cover a meeting of a group of garment cutters who were organizing themselves.

The meeting was in a small kosher restaurant on 17th Street, between 3rd and 4th Avenues. It had been warm when my father left Harlem that afternoon and he had not worn a coat, but as darkness fell it turned cold and a stiff wind was sending newspapers skittering along the empty street as he walked toward the restaurant, the collar of his suit jacket turned up against his neck. A man in a lumberjack's plaid shirt stood lounging against the plate glass of the restaurant, a toothpick in his mouth.

"Morgenstern," the man said.

"Steinfeld, hello, you look like you're ready for heavy labor."

"I'm glad you could come," Steinfeld said. "Those shits at The Forward, they don't pay any attention." He was a big man with a sensitive face who drank coffee occasionally in the Cafe Royale with a thin actress he was in love with. In Galicia, my father knew, he had studied to be a doctor, but now he worked in the garment district, his quick fingers racing over patterns with a pair of scissors. He shrugged his massive shoulders. "Heavy labor, sure. This is no kids' stuff, you know."

There had been a strike in one of the sweatshops that abounded like blossoms off the stem of lower 7th Avenue, and

then, mysteriously, there was a fire in the building and two of
the organizers of the strike were arrested, charged with arson.
Steinfeld himself had avoided the police only by accident. The
fire was the work of gangsters, everyone knew, but fighting back
was no easy matter.

My father lit a cigarette and glanced up the street. On the corner, a light burned in a newsstand but the other shops were dark.
He would have liked to stand outside and chat with Steinfeld but
it was cold and he opened the door of the restaurant. "See you
inside." As he moved into the warmth and the clatter of voices
from the already crowded tables, he heard the sound of a car on
the street but thought nothing of it. The shot rang out just as
the door was clicking shut behind him and it didn't register
immediately; even when the glass shattered and Steinfeld's
shoulders crashed through toward him, he didn't fully understand
what had happened. Then there was confusion, shouting, a man
rushing past him, jostling him, knocking him sideways, and he
cut his hand on a piece of glass and found himself on his knees,
staring into Steinfeld's wide open eyes. What he remembered most
of that moment, even many years later, was the lack of surprise
in them.

His hand was still bleeding when he got home, hours later,
although he had tied a handkerchief around it. Taking notes,
telephoning, typing his story, there had been no chance for the
wound to even begin to glaze over. The handkerchief was stiff with
congealing blood and my father was attempting to take it off, his
head lowered, as he climbed the stairs, and he bumped into
Shmelke, who was standing at the top of the steps.

"That woman, she's here, what should I do?" Shmelke said
breathlessly. His massive ears were tinged with red along the rims
like warning signs, and his lips seemed bluer than usual.

"So?" my father said, elbowing past him. "Excuse me. What
woman is that?"

He went to the bathroom and snapped on the light, discarding
the bloody handkerchief in the toilet.

"You don't understand," Shmelke whined. He was standing
right behind him, his face pressed close to my father's shoulder.

"She's right here, in my infermal room."

"What's to understand?" my father said. He turned on the cold water tap and plunged his hand into the lukewarm stream. "You should be congratulated, Shmelke. A charming young lady, visiting you here in your own room, and at this hour, no less. Wonderful. You are to be congratulated and I do congratulate you. And wish you good luck." He was filled with the events of the evening and would have liked nothing better than to share them, again, with anyone interested, even Shmelke, but the man's single-mindedness irritated him.

"*Morgenstern*, sometimes I wonder how such a dope can manage to climb the stairs, let alone turn the knob on the door." He pulled his head back when he saw the expression that flashed across my father's face. "You'll excuse me, I didn't mean to defend. But this woman, she's got me in such a tizzle. This *svartze*."

"Oh, that woman," my father said, his eyes widening. "She's here?"

"Here? That's nothing. Here I could live with. It's who she's got with her that sends shavings up my spine."

"Her boyfriend?" My father turned off the water and held his hand up to the light to examine the cut. It wasn't very deep but the glass had severed a big vein, an artery, perhaps, and the blood wouldn't stop seeping out. "Her husband? Her mother?"

"Worse," Shmelke said gloomily. His belligerence had suddenly faded and he stared at the raw wound on my father's hand as if he were considering how a similar gash would look on his throat. "What happened to your hand?"

"It's nothing," my father said. All of a sudden, he wanted to speak no more of it. All he wanted was to go to his room, drink a whiskey, and lie on his bed in the dark, where he knew the sound of shattering glass would reverberate in his ears all morning long. "What is it, Shmelke?"

"She's pregnant."

"Oh, so that's it." My father turned back to his hand, wrapping toilet paper around it till it was bulky as a crumpled package.

Shmelke observed this in silence, pursing his lips like water wings bobbing in a rough sea. "You know, maybe, a doctor?" he blurted out finally.

My father looked up from his hand into Shmelke's face and was washed with a wave of disgust. He remembered the blank, stoical eyes of Steinfeld staring up at him and he felt, suddenly, very tired. "Sure, sure," he said. He brushed past Shmelke. "I'll see in the morning." He walked down the hall.

"And Morgenstern?" There was a plaintiveness in Shmelke's voice my father had never heard before and it made him stop, his hand on the knob of his own door.

"Yes?"

"You could talk to her, maybe?"

My father turned around. "Now?"

"Sure, now. She's in my room, waiting. She won't go. All night, practically, she's here. She won't give me any peace. And Mrs. Lowe...." He nodded toward the stairs.

"Waiting for what?" my father asked. "Talk to her about what?"

"Tell her about the doctor you know. Tell her about how safe and sure this doctor is, how they take preclusions and it's no more than getting your tinsels out, just a little cut and..."

My father didn't wait for him to finish. He went down the hall and into Shmelke's room without knocking. The woman was sitting on the bed, her knees together and her hands clasped on them like a schoolchild waiting to receive her lesson. "Hello," my father said. "My name is Harry Morgenstern, I live here, down the hall."

The woman looked up at him and blinked. She was a small, very dark girl, hardly out of her teens, with a pointy chin and shoulders that didn't seem to matter. Her face was so dark, my father couldn't clearly make out her features, but she seemed pleasant enough, though hardly pretty. There was a blue kerchief with little white flowers on her head. "Where's Louis?" she demanded. Her voice was small but strong, like a rain that seems innocent enough but wets you through.

"I'm right here, my little flower," Shmelke said from the

doorway. "My friend Morgenstern, the novelist, he's a man
of the world, believe me, to him this is nothing. He's seen this
sort of thing dozens of times." He made a snapping motion
with his fingers but they wouldn't connect and there was only
a rasping sound. "It's only a triffle."

My father sat on the bed beside the woman. She glared at
him but, after a moment, her gaze softened.

"Why don't you leave us for a moment, Shmelke? There's
a bottle in my room, help yourself." He had to fumble in his
pocket with his left hand for the key. They waited until the
door had closed, Shmelke's footsteps sounded in the hall, and
another door could be heard opening, then closing. Then my
father and the black woman looked at each other again.

"He's very stupid, our friend," my father said simply.

"Ain't no friend of mine, not any more," the woman said.
"But stupid, that's for sure."

"I'm not the man of the world Shmelke says I am," my father
said, smiling, "But I can see trouble."

"I've got plenty to see." The skin on the woman's cheekbones
was so tight it glistened.

"What's your name?"

"Adrianne."

"That's nice," my father said. "That's a nice name."

The woman began to cry, lifting her hands to cover her face,
the sobs coming soft but steady for over a minute while my father
looked away and said nothing. When the sobbing became
inaudible, he said: "You don't want him."

"I know that, mister. I *acted* the fool, but I ain't no fool."

"What *do* you want?"

"I don't know. I came here thinking I wanted one thing but
now I don't know."

"A doctor?"

"A butcher, you mean? No, thank you, mister. I don't want
no coat hangers and razor blades in me. Bad enough what I let
get into me in the first place."

"Take it easy," my father said. "I'm not Shmelke. I just
asked."

"I'm sorry," Adrianne said.

They were quiet for a moment. My father looked idly at his hand. A muted red stain was beginning to spread through the toilet paper wrapping like fog spreading through the streets in the Cleveland evening, a lifetime ago. "Does Shmelke have any money?" he asked.

"That man?" She snorted. "He spends every cent on whiskey and such with his fancy friends downtown."

"I can give you some money, if it would help."

"It would," Adrianne said simply. It was clear she wasn't asking, but she wouldn't refuse.

My father stood up. "What about him?"

The woman shook her head sadly. The whites of her eyes were pink now, and her face was blurred, as if it had let go of the bones beneath the skin. "I don't want to see that poor excuse again."

"Wait here," my father said. He went across the hall to his room, hesitating just for a second before opening the door. Shmelke was sitting on the chair beside the bed, an empty glass in his hand. His reddened ears seemed to flap, like flags of distress.

My father knelt beside the bed and took some money from its hiding place in his suitcase. There wasn't much.

"What are you doing?" Shmelke asked. His voice was tiny, like that of a punished child.

"Saving your life," my father said.

"What do you mean?"

"What the thunder do you think I mean?" my father snapped. I know his temper, and I can imagine the way his eyes must have darkened, his moustache bristling. "Her father and brothers would kill you. I'm buying that off. But there's one condition. You can't let them find you. You'll have to leave."

Shmelke was speechless, but when my father glared at him, showing no sign of relenting, he said finally: "I'll go tomorrow."

"Tonight would be better, but it's your neck."

"I'll go early. There are things I have to do, circumcisions I have to attend to...."

"You know I don't mean just from here. I mean from New York."

"I know," Shmelke said bitterly. "I'm not stupid."

My father started for the door. Blood was beginning to drip on the bills he held in his bandaged hand.

"I'll pay you back," Shmelke said.

"If you want."

"I pay my debts, Morgenstern. I don't like to be a belcher."

My father shut the door and stood in the hall for a moment, staring at the money in his bloody hand. It was all he had, but that didn't mean anything.

The following year, my father was keeping company with a woman who might have become my mother, had he been a little less demanding. Years later, he liked to tell stories about this woman, whose name was Sarah, and kid my mother that he had settled for the daughter of a fanatic when he could have had a physician for a father-in-law.

My father was living in Coney Island at that time, in the same tiny apartment he and my mother would share their first year together, but Sarah's family was one of those which still maintained a handsome brownstone just north of 125th Street, a home with rich carpets on the parquet floors and servants living in the coach house. So, although he no longer lived there, he was a frequent visitor to Harlem, and he had occasion, once or twice, to pass Adrianne on the street or in the park. She had gone south, to stay with relatives, and had had her child. It was still there, with an aunt, and she was back, living with a man who fixed shoes in a small shop on 125th a few blocks east and tending the infant of a white family, taking it in its stroller for airings in the park, where the sun filtering through the newly opened leaves dappled the grass and benches with blotches of light and dark like footprints in the snow. My father, running across her with the stroller parked beside her bench, her uniform crisp and neat on her small, unremarkable form, paused to admire the infant, inquire about the other and shake his head sadly.

"It don't bear thinking about much," Adrianne said, and he agreed. There was no mention of Shmelke.

One Saturday afternoon in June, my father and Sarah took a short cut through the park on the way to Columbia University, where they planned to attend a free concert. As they walked, my father was suddenly arrested by a strange sight. A tall man wearing an overcoat was sitting on a bench under a chestnut tree, his ears big as the leaves hanging above his head. The overcoat was buttoned, although it was a warm day, and its collar was raised. The man wore dark glasses and there was a shapeless moustache over his bluish lips.

My father put his hand on Sarah's arm and steered her to a bench some fifty feet beyond the one where the man with the moustache sat, but facing it. "What is it?" Sarah asked. My father shooshed her with a finger to his nose. He crossed his legs and lit a cigarette.

Several people passed by, including a black nursemaid with a stroller and two small boys in short pants in tow. She wore her hair in braids and her silvery voice rose through the air like a bird's song as she chastised the lagging boys. They passed on, toward the far side of the park.

Before my father's cigarette was half gone, the man with the moustache, who had been nervously turning his head to and fro, became aware of the couple watching him and he bolted to his feet and began to hurry away.

"Wait here," my father said. He had to run to catch up with the tall man's quick strides.

"Shmelke."

"For God's sake, Morgenstern, my life is in jalopy, keep your voice down."

My father took him by the arm and gestured around. They were alone on a path that led through a small clump of trees. On the street, a hundred yards beyond, a fire engine raced by, its bell clanging. "Look, there's not a soul in sight. You're in no danger."

"I can't be too careless," Shmelke said.

They sat down on a bench.

"That false moustache is ridiculous," my father said. "Why didn't you grow a real one?"

"I was going to, but my wife didn't like it. It scritched," he said with disgust, as if describing some loathsome insect crawling on his face.

"Your wife?" my father asked.

"In Dayton."

"I heard you went back to Cleveland."

"Are you crazy, Morgenstern? Only to get some clothes."

"And in Dayton?"

Shmelke's lean shoulders had to struggle against the weight of the overcoat to produce a satisfied shrug. "Not so bad, not so bad as you might think. I'm in business there, producing plays, bringing artists in, musicians, travelling shows, let me tell you, Morgenstern, what Dayton has for culture, you could put in there." He raised a thumb, examined it critically, then replaced it with a pinky. "No more than that. In Dayton, they got taste in their elbow."

"And you're married?"

"Well....not exactly married," Shmelke shrugged again, the tips of his ears flaring. "Bedthroned. The happy day is next week."

"And what brings you here, Shmelke? Taking your life in your hands."

Shmelke sighed deeply, the breath rattling through his chest like a cold wind through dead branches, and the brown caterpillar beneath his nose wiggled, one end hanging loose. "There was....there was something I wanted to see. With my own eyes."

"Yes?"

"I wanted to see if....my wife, the woman to whom I'm intended, that is, Hindel, she would like to have children."

"So?" my father said. He took out a cigarette and lit it, wishing he had a bottle so he and Shmelke could share their ritual drink.

"So," Shmelke said, spreading his arms, "so I'm not such a thing of beauty, you know, but....and Hindel, well, she is a wonderful woman, but...." His voice trailed off and he looked over my father's shoulder, as if for inspiration in the trees.

"But what does all this have to do with your coming here?" my father asked.

"I wanted to see if.....you know, Morgenstern, if the child looks like me."

"It doesn't have a moustache, if that's what you mean," my father said. Immediately, he regretted having said that. If there was one thing he had learned in the long years it had taken him to come this far, it was not to hurt people, that it always came back to him if he did.

Shmelke took off his dark glasses and my father saw there were tears in his grey, almost colorless eyes. There was no surprise in them, though, as if the man who possessed them had become accustomed to rebuff. He clasped my father's hand and squeezed it, and for the first time in many months the place where it had been cut began to hurt.

"Is it so wrong, Morgenstern, for a man to want to see his own springoff? His own child? His own flesh and bones?"

"No," my father said. He disengaged his hand and got to his feet. Sarah would be wondering where he had gotten to.

Shmelke made a little sound in his throat and lowered his head, looking to his oversized feet for an answer that had eluded him so far in Cleveland and Dayton and would not easily be found here, either downtown on East Broadway or uptown in Harlem, where some people say the air is thinner.

My father didn't mention the money still owing, and neither did Shmelke.

A CHANGE OF LIFE

The summer he was thirty, a strange depression took hold of Skinner and held fast to him, like deep snow around a spinning tire.

It was easy enough to blame it on his age, the way Myrna did when she caught him moping, but he knew there was more to it than just that. Turning twenty-two had been *traumatic*; this was something else. He was beginning to drift, from Myrna, the children, his job, away even from himself. He sat at his desk in the study he'd finished paneling that spring, smoking cigarette after cigarette, taking stock of his life, writing out in his steady, careful hand meticulous balance sheets on special paper he brought home from the office. When his wife came upon him there, bringing a fresh cup of coffee, he smiled wanly. He was *glad* to see her, always, but never sure why.

The pieces of paper piled up in crumpled balls in his wastepaper basket and amounted to little more than that. On the plus side, there was the house and the mortgage obtained before the rates went sky high; the job he went to each day, where he performed specialized tasks that were easy for him; a small but steadily growing portfolio of stocks; Myrna herself, of course, and the children, little Andy, who everyone said had his father's eyes, and Mandy, who had Myrna's nose. On the debit side, there was the dubious factor of his age; the mortgage, high enough as it was; the car payments and the car repair bills; a tendency for a pain to lodge itself sullenly in his lower spine when the weather was bad; eyesight deteriorating so rapidly that he had been forced to change his prescription twice within as many years; and the leak in the washing machine which, despite his most determined efforts, hung on like a bad summer cold.

Little consolation in lists.

His work took him out of town much of the time and he found himself spending those useless hours above the clouds staring out of his window at the patchwork terrain below. He longed to see men as tiny as matchsticks bustling to and fro, displaying the meaninglessness of their existence, but at that altitude nothing of the sort could be deciphered from the spinning, panoramic puzzle which presented itself to him. Cloud banks drifted lazily across the screen of his vision, obstructing the view, without his noticing, so rapt was his scrutiny.

In other scraps of time, he read newspapers, a chore he had for many years fended off, again seeking a clue. But the symmetry of newsprint, while equally engrossing, was no more rewarding than that of the aerial maps which scribbled themselves across the frame of an airplane's window, constantly changing.

Myrna was no help. Her grandmother had influenced her life greatly and she tended to think that all things would pass. She was kind enough, though, not to chide him.

"The Brownlees are coming for dinner Thursday next," she said to him as they sat before the fire in the livingroom. She was mending one of the bright little things she'd made for Mandy.

"Mmmmmm," Skinner said, smiling attentively over the flap of newspaper which perched in his lap. An elderly man, a retired shingle manufacturer, had killed his wife in Syracuse by luring her to the roof of their suburban home, ostensibly to demonstrate a new shingling device he had invented in his spare time in the basement, and then pushing her to the rosebeds below. Skinner scrutinized the photograph in the paper carefully. The former shingle manufacturer was being arraigned on the murder charge and was flanked by two men, one a burly Negro detective, the other unidentified. The sudden widower was staring at the camera, a startled but half-amused expression on his face, as if he had been expecting the photographer but had not known from which dark corner he would spring. His lips were curled into an attempted smile, not nearly as neatly executed as the murder had been. There was something vaguely familiar about the man and Skinner rolled the face around in his mind, the way a child rolls a gumdrop in his cheek, but with no success. The name, of course, meant nothing to him.

"I said, how does that sound to you?" Myrna said sharply.

"I'm sorry, dear, I was watching that log crack."

She looked at him intently, then turned to glance at the log. It was just about to break in two. "The chicken sofflé," Myrna said.

On another occasion, after the children had been bathed and put to bed, they were playing cards with neighbors, Fred and Louise Tarrafly, on the screened porch. It was September, but the heat of the unusually warm summer lingered on. A Japanese lantern glowed softly overhead.

"Dummy," Louise said.

"Trump."

"Pass."

Three men had been sent into orbit in a lunar module capsule mounted on a Saturn 5 rocket, reported to stand thirty-seven storeys high, just that afternoon. According to the newspaper Skinner read before dinner, a new form of dehydrated food was being tested. There were to be no crumbs. On previous flights, the paper said, crumbs had proven to be a hazard, floating about in the weightless atmosphere, getting into things. The experimental food had been developed at a cost of $40,000. Computed at three meals a day, for three men, for the expected eleven days of the flight, that came to ninety-nine meals, for a cost of $404.04 per meal. Skinner frowned. It was too much.

"I said, your move, Ace," Fred said.

"Of course," Skinner said. "I was just trying to decide."

In the first week of October, Skinner's supervisor called him into his office. A slightly stooped man in his fifties, with a perpetual expression of kindliness on his thin lips, Louver had been in his position for close to ten years and knew quite well he would go no higher. He had, therefore a feeling of ambivalence toward the younger men, most of whom were brighter and more aggressive than he, who worked under him—at once he was concerned, almost fatherly, that they should not become trapped as he had been, and resentful that they would not be.

"I hope you won't think that I'm prying," he said, leaning back expansively in his swivel chair and locking his hands across the slight paunch which pressed against his alligator-skin belt, "but, I guess what I'm doing *is* prying." He tittered nervously, sent his chair into a skittish motion with a light flick of his foot and lit a cigarette, offering Skinner one.

Skinner leaned forward to accept the light and found himself, for the briefest of moments, looking up into hazel eyes. "Sir?" he asked cautiously.

"What I mean is, Jim, is there anything wrong? Troubles at home? Financial problems? Anything of that sort? Like I say, I don't mean to pry, but....." Louver's voice trailed off like a cry muffled by snow. He moved his soft mouth wordlessly.

In the short silence which followed, Skinner considered the questions already asked with care, drawing slowly on his cigarette. Anything wrong? Troubles at home? Financial problems? For a moment, he couldn't remember. Then he shook his head.

"You know, I've been married..." Louver began, but Skinner had already started the process of responding, and it was too late to stop. "No, I don't think so, sir." They both laughed nervously at the collision of words. "At least, none that I know of," Skinner added finally.

Louver swiveled his chair restlessly, his lips forming a fragile frown around the filtertip he clenched in his teeth, and Skinner felt guilty suddenly, knowing that his answer had been disappointing.

"Well, of course, if you don't want to level with me..." the supervisor said softly. His voice quivered the way young Andy's had, last year, when he said "thank you" to his Aunt Alice for the book he received on his birthday.

"I have been having a lot of trouble with my back," Skinner blurted out hopefully. Then he added, somewhat apologetically, "If that's the kind of thing you had in mind."

Louver's pudgy, closely shaven face brightened. He brought his chair to a sudden halt and leaned forward across his desk, wagging his finger in Skiner's face, like a schoolmarm who has caught you at it. "Aha," he exclaimed, a vindicated man. "I *knew* there was something."

It was agreed upon that, while Skinner's work had not actually been deteriorating, there had come to Louver's attention several small but nevertheless telling deficiencies in recent reports. The supervisor also took pains to cite several instances when he had noticed Skinner, sitting at his desk, pencil poised in the air, a distracted look on his face, gazing off into space. Even the secretaries had noticed that *something* seemed to be troubling him, Louver confided. Skinner lowered his head in submissiveness.

It was arranged, therefore, that Skinner would be dispatched to the Vancouver office to attend to some loose ends which had popped up there, due to the retirement of a senior official who apparently had been senile for several months immediately prior to his disengagement from the firm. The change in climate would be good for him, Louver was sure, and the job would really be quite simple; the month or so on the coast would really be more of a vacation than an assignment.

"No need to take the little woman along," the supervisor winked. "A month isn't all that long." Then he added, his cheeks flushing imperceptibly, "Unless, of course, you want to."

Skinner had been in Vancouver many times on business and it was one of his favorite cities, but it held no attraction for him now. It was raining on the day he arrived and it continued to rain. A tightness had developed in his chest, moreover, causing him no pain but making him frequently uncomfortable. He would have thrown himself into his work but Louver's prediction was correct and the job really was ridiculously easy, requiring hardly any of his time, just his presence.

He had rented a car, and the motel accommodations his motor club had arranged for him left little to be desired. He kept a modest supply of whiskey bottles in his room and a carton of cigarettes in the top drawer of the dresser, next to the dusty Gideon's Bible.

The first few days he was there, he was overcome by an intense loneliness, peculiar for a man who was so often away from home for several days at a time, and he wrote long, chatty letters each evening to Myrna, making sure to send along his love to the children. Then, that first weekend, with nowhere to go and nothing to do, he sat in his room for several hours and wrote a dozen letters as the rain slanted its way across the window. Each letter dated several days apart and all saying essentially the same— the weather was awful, it was dull here, the work was going along splendidly, you are all missed terribly. Then he addressed as many envlopes, sealed and stamped them and arranged them neatly on the dresser in the order in which they were to be mailed. He felt as if a great weight had been lifted from him—but, even as he stood smiling at his handiwork, he was washed over by a wave of guilt that made him weak.

He went for a drive in the rain, with no destination in mind. He went south, toward the Washington border and across it, and found a back road that led to the coast and further south along its craggy, winding shoulder. He drove until it was almost dark and he was tired, and pulled off onto a dirt road which disappeared finally in sand, a pebble's throw from the surf. He took off his shoes and socks, rolled up the cuffs of his pants and placed his feet gingerly onto the damp, clammy sand.

The rain had evaporated into what was little more than a mist, so vague that Skinner was barely aware of it. His cashmere cardigan grew moist as he walked and a damp lock of hair fell over his eye. The night was shrouded with low-hanging clouds and the sea itself was invisible; only the gurgling of gentle waves lapping discreetly against the sands, and the stinging scent of salt and rotting fish which assailed his nostrils told him it was there. At last, after timid steps, his feet were embraced by the chilly waters and Skinner stood, stock still, silent, his arms outstretched to the starless void which threatened to engulf him, a shoe and dangling sock in each hand.

A bird whirred past him, a seagull as big as a small dog, its white breast luminescent as a lighthouse beacon, and Skinner cried out loud, first in fright, then with pleasure. "Hey, you," he called after the gull, "it's me, Skinner. Who're you?" But the bird was gone as suddenly as it had come and Skinner was left talking to himself, feeling foolish. He sucked air into his lungs, thrusting out his chest and noticing that the tightness he'd felt there for days had lifted. "It's me, goddamn it, Skinner," he shouted, at the top of his voice.

He stood like that, arms outstretched, his head back, staring up at the grey, sullen sky, until his teeth began to chatter, and then he hurried back to the car, sliding into the seat, slamming the door, snapping on the heater, wriggling into his socks, squeezing into his shoes, lighting a cigarette—all in one flurry of motion. Then he heaved himself back wearily in his seat and toyed restlessly with the plastic knob on the end of the gear shift. He felt as if he were *close* to something, to some answer which had been eluding him, but he was uncertain as to the question, and completely unsure of which way to go. He had difficulty backing the car up in the deep sand and almost became stuck.

On his way back north, he stopped at a roadside cafe for a cup of coffee. The place was all but deserted—just a tired looking waitress behind an imitation walnut counter and the occasional sexless rumblings of someone behind the swinging doors marked "in" and "out."

The waitress ignored him but Skinner took note of her hips as she swished through the "in" door, then turned his attention to a grease-stained, dog-eared menu propped against a sugar bowl, its plastic cover intricately cracked. He was still glancing over the menu, his eyes unable to progress beyond the line advertising *Delicious, meaty hamburger, topped with meltingly delightful cheese and garnished with onion and pickle,* when the waitress reappeared and came to a stop before him. His eyes

were reading *hamburger, hamburger* over and over again, and there
was a slight pain at the base of his skull, as if, on its own, a slight
crack had appeared there, the beginning of an intricate pattern.
The tightness in his chest had returned, as stubborn as the stains
on the silverware the waitress put down with a gentle ''clink''
in front of him.

He raised his head slowly and looked at her—for a long moment,
they stared at each other, like former high school classmates who
meet by chance in a train station or lovers who, for the first time,
have reached an understanding—then he blurted out ''Coffee,''
his voice a shade too sharp, a little too sudden, like a hand darting
out for a hold when the feet fail. He opened his mouth again but
before the words came she was gone, down to the other end of
the counter where the coffee pot simmered, already pouring while
the sound of the order still rang in Skinner's ears.

''And a slice of apple pie,'' he said when she returned.

The waitress flared her nostrils and turned her face, frowning,
to a circular glassed container on a shelf halfway down the counter.
Inside, each on a separate plate, were several pieces of pie. She
was a blonde of some sort, bleached, Skinner supposed, with a
coarse, powder-caked complexion. ''No apple,'' she said. Her
accent was as flat as the counter.

Skinner studied her nostrils, which seemed to flare every time
she spoke or was spoken to. They were long and slender, very
neatly placed on the flat bottom of her slightly tilted nose, and
were immaculately clean—black, sculptured, quivering shapes,
more likely painted on than actual holes. ''Peach?'' he asked
hopefully.

She studied the pie display again, curling her upper lip above
a row of even, whitish teeth, the lower lip growing taut and
thin in a sort of smile. ''Uh-uh.'' She was closer to forty, he
suddenly thought, than the twenty-five or thirty he had first
supposed, but still youthful looking, slim, tight-bodied,
powerful. ''Cherry?'' he said after a moment's hesitation.

She put her left hand to her throat and pinched the flesh
beneath her chin with a stroking motion of thumb and
forefinger. There was no ring on her hand, he saw, and he knew

he had guessed right this time from the light which seeped into her eyes. "Okay," she said.

She had to reach up to get the pie, and bend forward, and Skinner watched her breasts, tugging against the thin cloth of her uniform, then her legs, which showed traces of what seemed to be soot around the calves but he supposed was grease. Her legs were slim and tight. He was hungry and he wolfed down the pie before bothering to put cream and sugar in his coffee.

The clock above the pie display case said 9:45, Coca Cola time, and Skinner was surprised, simultaneously, by how early it was, and how late. He was past-midnight tired but, on the other hand, it had still been light when he'd left his motel and he'd done no more than go for a drive. He looked around the desolate cafe— the atmosphere of the smoky, almost silent roadhouse was three-in-the-morning. Outside, the rain had begun again and it plowed dirty, corrugated trails through the sullen dust on the plate glass windows behind him. The booths were covered with peeling, reddish-maroon plastic, just a slight shade brighter than the Formica coating on the counter. The waitress, a wisp of dusky blond hair trailing in her eyes, was wiping glasses, looking tired, one hip thrust easily against the counter, watching the clock.

"Could I have a little more coffee?" Skinner asked.

"Okay." The woman moved easily, almost with grace, her whole body in motion as she glided down the length of the counter to where the coffee pot steamed and back. She poured with hardly a glance at his cup.

"When do you get off?" Skinner said, didn't ask, his voice directed toward the stream of flowing coffee, which stopped abruptly, just in time.

"Ten." The corner of her lip began to curl into a lopsided smile, then checked itself. She looked at him wearily.

"How about a date?" he said, looking up, admiring her nostrils, noticing with an absurd flush of pleasure that her eyes were hazel, like his own.

"Okay." She turned from him, the smile still incomplete, returned the coffee pot and busied herself with some dishes. Skinner sipped his coffee and watched the clock, trying not to think, not to think of anything.

At ten, punctually, the waitress removed her apron and disappeared through the swinging doors. Skinner could hear the soft murmur of voices—hers, perhaps, a high, feminine buzz, and a second voice, lower, darker, indeterminable—above the sudden clatter of dishes. Then the voices dropped off and he heard the spattering of fat. He imagined a slab of bacon hitting the griddle, immediately beginning to curl, the way her upper lip did when she smiled. Then there was a sharp laugh but he couldn't tell if it was hers. She reappeared, still in uniform but with a tan raincoat around her shoulders and a paisley scarf covering her hive of hair like a tent. He heard the click of her heels on the linoleum floor and he knew, without looking, that she had changed her shoes.

"Shall we go?" His voice sounded strangely polite and he almost extended his elbow to her.

"Okay?"

"Would you like a drink?"

"Okay?" Her answers had irritatingly become more like questions.

"I don't know my way around here, this area. You'll have to direct me." He was trying not to sound so formal, but he couldn't help it. His heart was pounding but in his mind he was with a business associate, on the way out of the office for lunch.

"Okay?" she said, the question mark at the end of the word grating against his ear.

Then he thought it best to say nothing.

She directed him to a dark, cheerless roadhouse several miles up the highway from the cafe, where the booths and tables seemed to be covered with the same peeling plastic, although, in the dim light of the cavernous, square-shaped room, it was hard to detect color. The smell of grease, perhaps floating on her skin, had followed them and it seemed to Skinner that the bar was merely an extension of the restaurant, another room in a desolate, depressing complex. The place was hardly more crowded than the cafe had been—a handful of awkward looking couples were adrift in the sea of tables, sheltered by the darkness and the high backs of booths. The tuneless blaring of the jukebox seemed no different than the clatter of dishes—to Skinner, both instruments played the same song. He and the woman barely spoke, letting the music intrude, gratefully.

Her apartment, then, was still another logical extension of the maze he had somehow fallen into. They had gotten there simply by his saying, during a pause of silence as records changed, "Why don't we go to your place?" and her answering "Okay" in her tired, noncommittal voice, and then a silent drive, first further down the highway, then off on a side road, then into a small town. She directed him with gestures of her restless hands. The collar of her coat was up and her head had shrunk into it.

She lived above a hardware store, at the top of a whitewashed outside stairway. Skinner kept his eyes on the street below as they climbed the stairs, but there was no one in sight. The rain had turned colder, almost to sleet. She turned on the lights in the livingroom as they entered and gestured toward the frayed, overstuffed chesterfield, then went directly to the bathroom. He didn't sit, but wandered around the room, examining its contents with one eye, searching for an ashtray with the other. Besides the chesterfield, there were two chairs, all part of a matching set, once probably something of value, and an assortment of tables— coffee tables, end tables, magazine racks, enough to make it difficult to walk through the room.

On the walls were half a dozen pictures—cheap prints, the kind you can buy, though Skinner never had, in any dime store; one showed a madonna, her eyes heavy with sleep, and a pacific child, their skins imbued with an unholy, pallid light; another depicted a mother cat licking the slicked fur of her squirming babies; above the chesterfield was a woodland scene, vaguely reminiscent, as if he had seen it a thousand times on the covers of newspaper supplements. There were a number of trees surrounding an oddly shaped pond, a field and a silo in the distance, ducks crowding at the edge of the water. Skinner was staring into the pond, feeling himself sinking beneath the turgid surface of the water, his cupped hand filling up with cigarette ash, when she returned.

"Hey?"

He turned, startled—he hadn't heard the bathroom door open or the sound of her footsteps. He glanced automatically downward and saw she was barefoot, that fact registering in his mind at the same time he realized that, in every other way, she was still dressed, only the raincoat was missing. He had hoped she would return to him naked, allowing him to avoid the awkwardness and tedium of undressing her. Still, there was something exciting about the way the smudged white uniform fit her, tight at the hips, slippery over the thighs. He started toward her, then realized that both his outstretched hands were filled with parts of cigarette, and stopped, his mouth hanging open.

"How do you like..." she was starting to say.

"I couldn't find an ashtray," he apologized.

"Oh, here." She turned and lifted a half-full black plastic bowl from a coffee table, where it had been all along, partially hidden by the open pages of a magazine. She offered it to him like a gift. "How do you like my place?"

He didn't say the first word that came to mind, startling him, but glanced around the room appreciatively, nodding his head, and finally said, "It's nice. I like it. I was admiring the painting here..." His voice trailed off. He put the ashtray down, his cigarette stubbed out in it, and took her in his arms. She came to him with the same passivity and indifference with which she had brought him his pie. They kissed, first slowly, almost shyly, then with determined seriousness, then excitement. She led him into the bedroom, already undoing her buttons, and within seconds he was on her, in her, through. His feet were cold but he ignored them. She was another matter—she lay like sand beneath him, soft, firm, unyielding, making his shape her own motionlessly. He stared past her ear, the swirl of hair above it, into the darkened cave the pillow formed. For a moment, he knew, he had been close to something, but he had let it slip by, untouched. "I'm sorry," he said after a while.

"It's okay," she said.

The following morning, Skinner sent a wire to his wife: "Myrna darling, something has come up, must see you, please come immediately, not the children, love Jim."

Before noon, impatient, he called her. Over the miles of wire, her startled voice sounded beyond reach. "Did you get my telegram?" he asked.

"Is this really you, Jim?"

"No, of course not, you couldn't have. I just sent it a little while ago."

"I mean, it's the middle of the day." Already, Myrna was beginning to whine.

"Listen, Myrna, you'll be getting a telegram soon..."

"Is everything all right?"

"A telegram, I just sent it a few hours ago, you should be..."

"What's the matter, Jim, what's happened?"

"Nothing, nothing's happened, everything's all right, everything's okay. Just something has come up and I want to talk to you about it right away."

"Jim, what is it, please tell me now." Her voice, suddenly, was very close, uncomfortably so, and very serious.

"No, it's nothing I can talk about on the phone. Now listen, Myrna, send the children to your mother's and get the first plane. I've checked, there's one at four fifteen. Can you take care of everything by then?"

"I think so, but Jim..."

"Good. If anything goes wrong, call me, I'm at the office, you have the number. If not, I'll be at the airport to meet you."

"Jim..."

"Give my love to the children, and to your mother. I'll see you soon, darling. Don't worry, it's nothing serious. I just have to talk to you. It'll be fun, you could use a holiday anyway. I love you, goodbye."

He hung up before her voice, which hovered ominously for a moment in the vast abyss between them, could accommodate itself to the machine-gun rapidity of his, and left the office immediately, fleeing the phone.

He was at the airport an hour early and stopped in the lounge for a beer. The dark, mirrored room was almost empty—besides Skinner and the morose bartender, there were only two other customers. One, a tall, solemn looking man with the polished elbows of his tweed suit on the polished bar, was bent over a newspaper turned to the stocks. The other, a thin, greyish woman with a wen on her neck, was in the booth behind Skinner, her image in the bar mirror forlorn and flat as she sipped slowly and politely at a glass of beer. She looked up to meet Skinner's stare and smiled, first sheepishly, as if she had been caught in some compromising act, then knowingly, as if she and the stranger who studied her reflection shared some deep, hidden joke. There was something vaguely familiar about the woman and, after a moment, Skinner thought he could see through the wrinkled, shallow skin of her shrunken face the fuller cheeks and features of the blonde waitress he had spent so much wasted time with the night before. He turned his eyes away.

On his way to the arrival gate he stopped at a gift shop and bought a box of Myrna's favorite candies. The plane was late and he stood with his shoulder against a wall, a tall, angular man with a blank face and dull hazel eyes, trying to remember why he had wanted her to come, what he would say to her. His shoulder was beginning to hurt and he had come to no conclusion when the bustle of passengers crowding into the arrival lounge roused him just in time to see his wife, last as always, emerge through the narrow gate, glancing about searchingly. There was something touching about her gesture, something that melted away all his irritation and forced him away from the wall, toward her.

"Myrna, here..."

"Jim, darling, what..." She was breathless and her hair was in disarray, as if, from the moment he had called her, hours earlier, she had been in constant motion. He took her by the arm, pecked at the flushed cheek she offered.

"Here," he said, pressing the rectangular box into her grasp. "Chocolate cherries."

They went for a drive. Skinner fended off her questions as he manoeuvered the rented car through the early evening traffic and out of the city, heading south. They crossed the border as Myrna was telling him what Mandy said when she bruised her knee.

"And then she didn't cry anymore. She's such an angel."

It was dark when Skinner pulled the car off the dirt road onto the sand, but he could see the tracks he had made the night before in his headlights, like smudges on glass. "Where are we?" Myrna asked, and Skinner replied cryptically: "A secret place." He held her by the hand as they walked across the packed sand to where the sea lapped gently against their feet. Myrna took off her low-heeled shoes and the bottoms of her stockings were drenched. The night was still, dark, heavy around them. The muted roar of the surf was soundless under the oppressive silence of the night itself.

"Come, don't be frightened," Skinner said. He sounded so solemn, like a character in a bad French movie, that he almost laughed himself but he was thinking too fast to waste the time it would have taken to explain. He took her by the hand and led her deeper into the hissing water—up to their ankles, then their knees, like cold and lonely Baptists. The bottoms of his pants legs clung coldly to his calves, like fingers pressing hard against the skin. "I came here last night," he began slowly, "and I realized something for the first time. I had to tell you." But even as he said the words he realized with a hard clarity that he had nothing to tell, that he had learned nothing except his voicelessness.

Myrna clung tightly to his arm, leaned her head against his shoulder. "I'm glad you called, Jim. What is it? Tell me?" There was a softness to her voice he hadn't heard in years.

Something flew blindly past their heads—a bat, a bird, he didn't know what, but he jerked away from her suddenly, as if to take chase. She stumbled as his weight shifted out from beneath her, and, as her feet gave way, he was reeling suddenly, back to her, throwing himself on her, forcing her down, under.

"Gaaaaaaaaaa." He was screamimg, in rage, drowning out her cries of panic. Bits of his life spun before his eyes, though it wasn't he who was drowning—the face of the shingle manufacturer, illuminated with surprise by the flashbulb; Louver's smoothly shaven, pink face flooded with ambivalence; the helmetted face of an astronaut, a satisfied smile behind the glass—and all the anger and motion which had been building in him for months erupted like a ripe tomato hitting a garden fence, funneling with dizzying force into his hands, pressing her down, killing her, wounding himself.

Then, just as suddenly as it had come, the spell lifted, like a cloud drifting away from the moon, illuminating the night. With a shudder, he jerked back, dragging her limply toward him. Her eyes were open and her lips were twisted into a vague smile from which a thin whimper stuttered. "Myrna, Myrna, I'm sorry," he sobbed, holding her tight to his chest, "I didn't mean to do that. I don't know what happened, I...." He buried his face in her wet hair but there was something there that seemed to reproach him and he pulled away from her, letting her fall to her knees.

Skinner stood there, suspended in time and motion, his feet frozen in the sand, his chest heaving, looking down at her, then up and along the narrow beach which stretched on forever, into darkness. His eyes followed the sweep of it out to sea. He turned and followed the line, thrashing his way through the waves until the water was up to his armpits, then he heaved himself forward and began to swim. Behind him, on the beach, Myrna was calling but her voice was drowned out by a whirring above his head. There was a cool gush of air on his cheek and he realized it was a seagull passing by—or maybe not, perhaps it was something else. It was gone, though, and he pursued it. There was more strength in his arms than he would have imagined. The tightness in his chest was gone and he gasped out an excited cry. He felt his lips curving upward into something of a smile, as if the bird could see.

RABBIT DONE RUN, SEYMOUR WENT AWAY AND ROSACOKE'S GOT THE BLUES

Bengtson slid down her pants and tried not to look.

She leaned against his desk. "Fuck the shit out of me," she said.

"Don't be vulgar."

"It's better than saying I love you, isn't it?"

That made him look at her face, closely. There was something soft there, softer than all the softnesses of all the women he'd ever known rolled together. You could choke on it.

"That *would* be vulgar."

He held her close to him and tried to ignore her nakedness, the cool feel of her skin through his tweed trousers, his shirt, his vest. This was something different than sex.

Over his shoulder, she watched the air filtering through the transom.

"Tell me again," Roxanne said. "Say it again, please."

They were lying on his desk, she on top of him so he wouldn't break her in half, his ass squashed flat against the blotter—thank God for *that* or he'd get a splinter for sure. She really was charming, he thought, so...*loving* was the word that formed in his mind but he spit that away.

"John Updike has a crooked nose."

She giggled. "Hawklike, it's *hawklike*."

"No, crooked. Hooked. He's Jewish, really, you know. His mother put him in a beer bottle in the Pennsylvania bullrushes during the Quaker pogroms of 1932. He was found by a graceful spinster, a second cousin to John O'Hara, I believe, on the doctor's side, who was washing out her pantyhose."

"No, no, tell me about Rabbit." She beat her little fists on his chest. The desk creaked under their force. He noticed, his nose buried in her hair, that the transom was open. Can they hear us in the hallway? he wondered. It was late, but janitors have big ears.

"Rabbit likes blow jobs."

"No!" She was getting too loud, and her mouth was slung into a pout. The pink of her lower lip shone. He muffled her with a kiss.

"Rabbit takes it in the ear," he whispered.

"They're big enough."

"Oh, that's bad."

"Well, you're the one who's blaspheming."

"It's no blasphemy." His voice took on the steady, even tone reserved usually for the classroom. "When no one's looking Rosacoke blows Rabbit and Seymour watches. That's all he..."

She cut him off with her tongue. "Everyone's got to have heroes. Maybe they don't mean anything to you anymore, but don't spoil them for me."

"Hey." He would have pulled his head back to look at her better, but there was nowhere for it to go. "I'm only kidding, you know."

But she could raise her head, and she did. There was something so earnest about the way she looked at him, her eyes devouring him. He was still in her and he felt himself stiffen. That made him think about how easy it had been *getting* in, but of course that didn't mean anything anymore. There was a poster on his door that his eyes strayed to, fell on for a moment, then moved on, back to the honey explosion of her hair: a green tree on a yellow background, a butterfly, and a quote from Bob Kennedy: *Some men see things as they are and say why, I dream things that never were and say why not.* But it was really Robert Frost who said that, wasn't it?

Roxanne went home at Christmas and didn't come back to school. Home was where Momma or Poppa happened to be at the time, not Halifax, where she'd spent her girlhood, anymore, or even Toronto, which she'd said at school was home because it was the last place they'd been before. Poppa's play had been bought by television and he was in Hollywood writing the script. Momma was in New York, in an apartment Roxanne knew nobody could possibly pay for, just off Washington Square.

"It's humiliating, actually," Victoria said. "Television. Stanley Lumut was interested, but Shelly insisted Peter hold out for more money. So now look what it's got him."

"More money?" Roxanne asked. The apartment had a fireplace, at least, and it was cozy curling up in front of it, just like on the farm, under the comforter Grandmum had made for her.

"Yes, yes, more money, of course..." Victoria frowned at her. She was sunk deeply into the white leather sling chair in which she felt most comfortable when on the attack. Shelly was Peter's agent, a man for whom she had the most profound contempt. Fifty percent of his ten percent should have been hers. There was a reason Roxanne had come home for Christmas, even though earlier plans had called for them to meet, later in the week, at Lake Louise or Aspen, wherever the snow was better. She would get to it in a moment.

"But that's not the point, dear." Smoke streamed from Victoria's nostrils. Roxanne watched the clean suck of air in the fireplace, the rising of the heat. "The point is, your father should not be writing for television."

"Why not?" Roxanne asked. She was being irritating, she knew it, and couldn't help herself. She really didn't like the place, the teak furniture, the wrought iron that went nowhere, the seventeen ceramic or glass ashtrays—she had counted them that morning—all for one person who smoked, although she did smoke too much. She had sent a telegram begging off the skiing and asking for the farm, but since Grandmum's death Momma hadn't liked to go there.

"All right, girl, spit it out." Victoria was tired of playing, it was time to get down to business. "You're pregnant, aren't you."

Roxanne was taken off balance. She had rehearsed in her head how she would break the news. "Does it show already?" Her eyes were frightened and Victoria was touched.

"No, don't worry about your girlish figure." She frowned the obvious thought away. "I was seventeen once, too."

Roxanne drew her knees up under the comforter and hugged them, her chin on her arm. "Did you get pregnant when you were seventeen, Momma?"

Victoria blew smoke at the chandelier. "Some school we waste our money on. Your father wastes himself in television so we can afford this. They promise to take care of you and you come home pregnant. They promise to give you an education good enough to get you into Vassar or Smith and you can't even count. How old are you, child, and how old am I?"

"This is different," Roxanne said. "That was Poppa."

"Yes. Too bad your Grandmum didn't see it that way at the time." She doubled her cigarette in a porcelain tray and slid out of the chair onto the leopard skin. She had shot it herself, the year before, while Peter was in Spain writing the play. Africa had seemed so close. "Does he know?"

"Poppa?"

"Roxanne. Please don't play games with me."

"Oh. No."

"Are you going to tell him?"

"I don't think so."

"Is he married?"

"No."

They stared at each other, Victoria frowning, Roxanne blank and open, until the girl turned away. A log was cracking in the fireplace. The room was unsettlingly white, white walls, the white sofa, the white chair, the chandelier, and the black things in it only made the whiteness whiter, as if Momma were not to be cheated of snow.

"Is it one of your teachers?"

Roxanne blushed, couldn't help herself. She stared down at her hands. "I promised not to tell."

"Promised? Promised who?"

Roxanne mumbled.

"*Roxanne!*"

"I promised myself."

Victoria laughed, lit a cigarette with a gold lighter. "That's very noble, dear, but it doesn't pay the hospital bills."

"It's free at home."

"*This* is home dear, we're Americans now. Don't pout." She touched her daughter's hair, smoothed it away from her eyes. "We'll talk about it more tomorrow, after you've rested and had the good cry I can see is brewing."

She put her arms behind her and leaned back. Her hand touched the leopard's head and she rubbed the smooth curved teeth with her thumb. "Imagine, a teacher taking advantage of an innocent girl. If I tell Peter about it, he'll track him down and slice off his balls."

"I love his balls," Roxanne said. The crying began, as predicted.

"Yes, I can imagine," Victoria said.

During her confinement, Roxanne reread *A Long and Happy Life*, *Nine Stories*, *Rabbit, Run*, *Lord of the Flies* and, in fact, the entire reading list, including Fowles, whom she didn't like. She also read *Raise High the Roof Beam, Carpenters*, which hadn't been out long enough to be included but would be, in time, and *Imagine Kissing Pete*, which wasn't on the list either but was one of Bengtson's favorites, she knew.

She spent a lot of time staring at things—the fire, the embers, through the window, into the eyes of the leopard—and letting things form in her. She thought a great deal about something Bengtson had said in class one day, that stories didn't exist in a vacuum, they were part of the character of their creators, and that characters in stories were extensions of those same creators' characters. Who was the hero, then, she wondered: Seymour or J.D.?

"If you won't tell me his name, at least what's his birthday?" Victoria asked. They were sitting in the breakfast nook, where everything was green and the narrow passageway between the fridge and the pantry was choked with vines.

"What on earth for?" Momma had turned out to be better than Roxanne had hoped for, a good sport, and they could talk easily now, though there were still some secrets.

"So I can check his horoscope, naturally." *The Daily News* was on the glass table between them. Victoria read it for the columns.

"I don't know. February, I think."

"February? I should have known. Aquarius or Pisces? Well, it doesn't matter, the damage's been done." She thumbed through the paper. "Hah. If he's Pisces, as seems likely, domestic complications are interfering with his work today. Good, God is punishing him."

"You don't believe in God, Momma."

"It's just an expression. What's his first name?"

"Robert."

"Robert. I thought you said Rabbit."

"I did."

"Not a comment on his sexual proclivities, I hope. Rabbit and Roxanne, that's cute."

"And Rosacoke," Roxanne said.

"What?"

"Rabbit and Rosacoke. Honestly, Momma, don't you read books?"

"When I was your age, I was reading *Moby Dick.*"

"I read *that* in grade nine."

Alone in her room later, she dreamed: Rosacoke Bengtson took hold, feeling the curve of muscle beneath her hand, feeling the motion as the machine between her legs bent, leaned to the curve of the earth. It sounded good. Well, Roxanne Bengtson, that was all right too. But what a name to be saddled with. It was logical that a Victoria should have brought forth a Roxanne, she supposed. Rosacoke, *really*, would probably be worse. She kept wanting to think of names for the baby, but knew she shouldn't do that. Victoria told her not to think about it at all.

Roxanne ran into Bengtson at a Star Trek convention in New York.

"You don't remember me, do you?" Behind her sunglasses, her eyes appeared hurt.

"Of course I do. It's wonderful to see you. Are you a Trekkie?"

She laughed. "No, I'm a writer. Trying to be, anyway. Can you believe that? I'm doing a story for one of the Canadian newspaper supplements. And...are you?" She was talking too quickly, she knew, almost breathlessly.

"Not really. I'm sort of...an observer. Well, if you're a writer, I don't have to tell you about the sociological overtones. It's funny, I'm sort of covering it, too. I mean, I intend to use some of this in something I'm writing." He appraised the soft tightness of her cheeks, looking for a clue.

"Are you finally finishing your dissertation?"

He flushed. "Yes, how did you guess?" Bengtson's eyes were sharp. He had put on some weight, not much, and lost a little hair, but still looked rumpled and intense. Despite the extra weight, he looked less sturdy in denim than he had in tweed, less substantial. Roxanne herself was different, of course.

Elbows crowded in on them and there was an awkward silence.

"There must be a thousand people in the ballroom," Roxanne said.

"Why don't I buy you a drink?"

"All right, if we can find a place with a square inch of room."

They had to go to a different hotel for that, but not far enough away for the spell to be broken.

"You really don't remember me, do you?"

Bengtson shook his head. "I feel like an idiot. I know you were one of my students, but there have been so many...I'm sorry." He peered at her. It was funny. She had remembered his eyes as being brown, but they were blue.

TRESPASSERS WILL BE VIOLATED

The water of the quarry was dead. Slime and vegetation crept on the bottom like mold, sucking whatever life there might have once been from it. If you swam way out, Valerie said, you could feel the cool surge of some vague, hidden springs, but mostly the water had a tepid feel, and it left a foul taste in the mouth, as if it were slightly polluted. Brad didn't like it and he would have preferred to go to the lake, or even the rec centre pool in town, chlorinated or not, but she was in one of her moods—"I vant to be alone," she mugged, insisting, and he gave in.

The quarry was some five miles from town, on a narrow country road that branched off from the highway north of the campus. Another half-mile, just past a small bridge spanning a dried and caking stream bed, was a dirt trail, its mouth clogged by weeds; it led, winding and bumpy, to a wide clearing dominated by placid gravel heaps and, just beyond, another small bridge, its beams and planks weather-cracked. About a hundred feet past this bridge lay the quarry itself, and, since Brad was reluctant to attempt the crossing in his precious car, they always parked beneath the shelter of a grove of large, expansive trees—cottonwoods, he thought they were—and went the rest of the way by foot. Valerie complained of this but Brad shrugged it off, laughing.

"You don't give a shit about my feet," she said.

"That's true. From your ankles down, you're a loser. But go the other way, well then..."

She had, in fact, very small feet—they, her wrists and breasts were the only small, delicate parts of her body—and she was excessively vain about them. She was a large-boned girl of twenty, with a horsey jaw protruding from her basically attractive face and heavy eyes, man's eyes, really, piercing out from a gently curved forehead. Her calves were thick with the muscles of a girlhood filled with dancing lessons, and her hands were always discolored with paint.

From where he lay basking in the sun on the blanket they'd spread out on the one tiny stretch of sand along the narrow approach to the water, Brad could see the Healey cooling in the shade across the bridge, sunbursts spinning off the chrome of the hubcaps. He closed the paperback Kant he'd been only half-reading to study with pleasure the silhouette of his car and debate with himself whether it needed a washing. The Healey, old and battered, was the only material possession of any value Brad owned and the one which, come the revolution, they'd have to fight him for. He had discovered the quarry one Saturday afternoon in April of the past year when he was out on one of his solitary drives, exploring the web of back roads surrounding the town, and had adopted it as the perfect place to do his car washing—a weekly ritual. The spot was completely isolated, so he could turn his classical tapes up to top volume, and the sun beat down relentlessly, ricocheting off the gravel and limestone walls of the quarry, giving him an opportunity to put some tan on his usually pallid skin. It hadn't occurred to him to swim there, in that slippery warm water, but one day when Valerie was in town he had brought her with him and she'd been delighted, stripping and diving in despite his good-natured grumbling. He should have known, he'd reflected then, that she would love the place.

After that, he'd gone in a few times himself, when she was with him—although he insisted they wear suits, and she gave in on that—but he didn't like it much and preferred to spend their afternoons there washing the car, or studying, while she swam, at one with the steep, desolate pond.

The quarry was shaped like a spoon, with a long, narrow handle where the water was shallow and came right up, at the tip, to a rocky little stretch of shore that had once served as the entrance to the miniature canyon the quarry formed. Progressing through the handle, the water got deeper and the limestone walls rose higher until, once out in the middle of the spoon, the swimmer could look up and feel as if he were completely enclosed by the sheer rock. The quarry walls rose several hundred feet above the water level, and the water itself, Valerie had told him, was twelve or fifteen feet in its deepest parts. Brad assumed, although he didn't really know, that after the quarry had been abandoned—possibly because water was struck—the seepage, aided by rainfall, had taken over. Vegetation had flourished too; something akin to seaweed formed a ticklish carpet on the quarry's floor, and all manner of shrubs struggled through cracks in the gravel heaps and even along the crevasses of the limestone. The din of insects, at night, was insistent and vibrant.

Brad roused himself and got to his feet, shaking a charley horse out of his leg. Way out in the middle of the quarry's spoon, he could see Valerie methodically stroking. He stared for a moment, satisfied himself that she was all right, then turned and trudged up the path toward the bridge and the Healey.

By the time he'd returned, trailing against his leg the bucket he kept in the trunk, Valerie was sloshing her way through the shallow water of the spoon handle toward him. Rivulets of water were streaming from her two-piece suit—not quite a bikini—and from her hair, which hung in lank, shiny strands around her throat. Her breasts rose and fell with her heavy breathing and her somewhat broad shoulders were tinged with red. She looked quite beautiful—more so, Brad thought, than she'd seemed for some time—and a small twinge of passion tugged at him. He felt remorse for the way things had turned and impulsively resolved to himself that everything could be saved.

She slapped the water off her arms and legs, wrung out her hair and sprawled, gingerly, on the blanket face down as he stood watching, grinning at her. "Hi, babe," he said.

Valerie twisted one arm behind her to unhook the top of her suit, tossing it lightly aside. "The water is beautiful," she said. "Beautiful." She lifted her face to be kissed and Brad plopped down beside her gratefully. A vision of the previous night passed before his eyes but he put it aside.

He lit one of her cigarettes and placed it between her wet lips. With a hesitant hand, he caressed her damp, upturned face. There was a strand of pale green weed on her cheek that he gingerly lifted off. "I'm glad you missed that bus," he said. "I don't want you to go."

She didn't respond and he ran his hand down her neck to her breast, squashed almost flat against the blanket. With his other hand, he stroked the small of her back, finally slipping two fingers under the red and white striped bottom of her suit. Valerie shivered but he didn't stop. She kept her face turned to him, watching, but the light had fled from her eyes, like the sun darting from a wet pebble, leaving hard rock behind. He slid up against her and took her into his arms. As he groped with the zipper on the suit bottom he raised his head and glanced over his shoulder to reassure himself that no one was there, that they were alone.

"Don't, Brad, it's too hot," Valerie whimpered. He was having trouble with the zipper, jerked at it hard and pinched her skin. "Brad, you're hurting me," she cried. Then she turned her face away and didn't say any more. It wasn't rape—they had been too close for too long for that—but it was something he did by himself. Once he'd begun, Valerie lay quietly beneath him, her cheek resting on the blanket, her eyes climbing, then descending, then climbing again the limestone wall to the north of the quarry. It went very quickly, and he was silent except to say "Goddamn it" when he lost control. He rolled heavily off her and lay on his back staring at the dizzying sun, struggling against a pain just behind his eyes. Sun spots scattered off the leaves fluttering above them like rain drops on the Healey's windshield. Valerie's cigarette, which he'd placed on a rock, was still burning and he put it in his mouth, took a deep drag and crinkled his nose around the jagged smoke.

They lay silently beside each other for a long time—what seemed

to him like a long time—until his shoulders began to ache from
the pebbles embedded in the sand. "I'm sorry, Val," he said
softly, sitting up. As he said it, he wondered what he was sorry
for.

Valerie got up and brushed the sand from the back of her
legs. She walked to the water's edge and stood, feet immersed,
staring off across the quarry. Brad found himself admiring the
smooth flow of her back and shook his head violently.

"Did you enjoy that," she said coldly, without moving. The
sound of her voice surprised him, the suddenness of it, and the
thinness. It didn't sound like her voice. "I hope so. I hope you
enjoyed that. I certainly did." Then, without waiting for a
reply—none was coming—she sloshed a few feet into the water.

"Wait, Val, let's talk, eh?"

She ignored his feeble call and waded on, up to her knees.
She appeared to be going in slow motion, struggling against the
soft goo and slime at the bottom, sucking at her feet. The sun
shone in her still damp hair and Brad had to look away, shield
his eyes from the glare. He thought obliquely of an image in
the painting she'd been working on the night before—a woman
stuck to the pavement in an urban blur, struggling to move her
feet which are fastened to the street by invisible bonds as a crowd
looms up to engulf her, a cold steel sun burning overhead, like
dry ice. He'd stood behind her for a long time, his eyes shift-
ing randomly from the canvas to the woman who daubed at it,
until she'd snapped at him: "Do you have to stand right behind
me like that?" Rebuffed, he'd retreated. "I thought you came
here to visit me," he said, immediately ashamed at the hurt-
little-boy tone in his voice. But the canvas seemed to dominate
the room, and her discolored smock smelled foul. When she
didn't answer, the shame vanished and he shouted at her:
"Listen, if you don't like being with me, and it's obvious you
don't, why don't you get the hell out of here?" She cursed back
and threw a paintbrush at him. It landed with a sickly plop on
the sofa and Brad lunged for it. While he was wiping up the
fuchsia mess, she was telephoning the bus depot. Then they
had glowered at each other across the room. "There's a bus

out at 9:15," she said coldly. "I'm going to take a nap and then leave." She didn't wait for his reply, just turned and went into the bedroom. He saw her pick up the alarm clock and was struck by the absurdity of what was happening. It was *his* bedroom, not hers—she had never really been part of it; it was *his* alarm clock. "Jesus," he shouted and slammed out.

As soon as he'd gotten out on the street, his head cleared and he regretted it—everything. He knew she was going through hell at home, her parents making life miserable for her—partially because of him, he supposed. And it had something to do with him, too—perhaps he didn't love her anymore, perhaps he never really had. But he *felt* like he loved her—though he knew he didn't always show it. "Fuck"—he resolved to be strong. It was *she* who was acting like a child, not him. She could go to hell for all he cared—well, she could stew for a while. He went to the office he shared with another grad assistant in the English-Philosophy Building and tried to work on his thesis, but it was useless. Nevertheless, he forced himself to stick around, brewing a pot of tea, aimlessly tossing darts at the board pinned on the office door. At 9:30, he went to a tavern, thinking he might pick up a girl, if he could find one, which he didn't—and was relieved he hadn't when he got home, past 11:00, and found her, asleep, in her nightgown, on the living room sofa, one paint-smeared hand trailing on the floor, her wrinkled face close to the spot she had stained. She woke in his arms as he carried her to the bedroom, pushing her face silently, insistently against his shoulder.

"I thought you were leaving." He placed her gently on the bed and sat down beside her. He kicked off his boots.

"I overslept and missed the bus," she said tersely. He was pretty sure she was lying but he said nothing, he was so happy to see her, to be sitting quietly, so close. He remembered how, when he was a child, he could close his eyes and imagine anything.

She rolled over and put her face to the wall. When he turned off the lights and slid into bed beside her, he could hear her muffled crying through the pillow. He reached out a hand slowly and caressed the small of her back but she shuddered and he withdrew to his own side of the bed. "What is it?" he said, and after a long silence she replied: "Everything." But she didn't turn to him, and he stayed on his side of the bed. The heat in the apartment was terrific, pressing down on them like a stone, and for a long time he couldn't sleep despite the tiredness aching in his legs. They lay still, as if chained to the bed, as if some frightening barrier, some awesome creature or an electric wire, lay between them. Then, just as he was almost asleep, he felt her roll over next to him and place a soft hand on his shoulder. He pretended to be asleep.

He heard a splash and looked up. He couldn't see Valerie, just glare off the water where she had been a moment before, up to her knees. He jumped to his feet, a sudden panic striking him, and called her name. Shading his eyes, he could see her, swimming strongly, at the point where the handle opened up into the spoon of the quarry. The panic which had pulled him to his feet dragged him, quickly, unthinking, into the water. He called her name again, struggling through the slime, over and over again until he was in deep enough to begin swimming.

He was not an exceptionally good swimmer—surely no match for Valerie, who had raced in high school—and he didn't really enjoy water except for splashing around. Deep water, like heights and close quarters, was one of the many physical things which made him uncomfortable, just short of frightening him. His passion for the Healey, and speed, was a quirk in his personality, and he'd always admitted it. Now he wished he had that speed here, within himself. He knew he couldn't catch up with her, and he felt with certainty as clear as running water what she was planning to do—and that he *had* to catch her.

She was playing tag with him, in fact, heading in one direction, then diving deep, surfacing thirty feet away and starting off in another direction. She was way out in the centre of the quarry by the time Brad reached its opening, and already he was tired. His arms seemed like huge trunks of dead wood straining to sink and rest, longing to drag him down. He was in water way above his head and he stopped to tread water in a new panic.

"Val, for God's sake, stop playing," he shouted. "Val. *Val.*" He whirled around in the water, flaying with his outstretched arms. He couldn't see her anywhere. "Val. Valerie. Please, please. I love you. Val? Do you hear me?"

There was an echo in the quarry, and his words bounced off the high limestone walls and flung themselves back at him like shotgun pellets. Then there was silence and he strained his ears for a sound of her, anything. There was a splash suddenly, not more than a hundred feet from him, along one smooth stone wall. The water was deep there, and the stone was too steep, too smooth for anyone to climb. He treaded water, gasping for breath, and stared at the wall, then at the water separating them. There was a smooth, swishing sound, as if something were moving through the calm water. He searched the surface, where the rays of sun diffused in broad splotches, ominous streaks of weed waved and rings were beginning to spread. There was something out there, he was sure of it. He thought immediately of snakes, his skin turning cold, quivering. He had never seen any at the quarry, but he was sure that many snakes must live in the rocks, and he was always watchful for them. He looked down and his breath froze in his throat. Through the murky water, he could see his nakedness.

"*Val*," he screamed. "Val, stop fooling around. Damn it, Val, I'm tired...I'm going back." The echo spit his words back at him, "going back, going back" and he began to swim, dragging his heavy arms through the water, kicking with a fury. *Not me*, he thought, clenching his eyes shut, *not me*.

He dragged himself out of the water and lay panting on the blanket for several minutes, tears streaming down his cheeks, his body racked by coughs. Then, slowly, he rose and put on his trunks. "Val," he called, shading his eyes with a hand and peering out across the handle of the quarry. Shadows flickered on the water; he felt cold. "Valerie," he shouted. There was a faint echo, as if the cold limestone walls were mocking him. "Valerie," he called again, then repeated the name one more time, softly, to himself.

He followed the narrow path leading to the quarry's rim, brushing carefully at the weeds clogging the way. He walked along the edge, barefoot, drawing as close as he dared, calling her name.

There was a chance she was hiding somewhere, turning the tables on him, making him suffer—he didn't really believe that, but he kept forcing the thought to the front of his mind, an image of her flattened against the quarry wall, her face lifted as she followed him with hungry eyes, a queer, satisfied smile on her lips. He came to a spot where he could see almost the entire spoon of the quarry below him—the sheer walls, unbroken save for an occasional stubborn bush clinging to the stone, and the placid water below, unbroken. A thin shiver spread itself into a cold hand groping along his thigh as he stared down into the abyss. The sun was directly behind him, beginning to sink low in the sky, and it glistened on the smooth water, burnishing it like metal. For as far as the eye could see, there was no living thing.

He met them in the lobby of their hotel and they went to a restaurant to talk. Both Brad and Valerie's father would have preferred a lounge, but the presence of her mother, a pious-looking, grey-haired woman whose face Brad searched in vain for a clue to a connection with the daughter, seemed to eliminate that chip in the wall of rules and propriety which had surrounded him since the accident.

The parents had arrived the following day, tense and haunted looking, but kept to their room while the quarry was being dragged. Brad supposed that, during that agonizing two days, they lived in some sort of stupor, not really believing their daughter was dead—there was no real proof she had drowned, after all—but not really daring to believe she was alive. Brad himself wouldn't allow a complete surrender, knowing that the kind of cruel joke this would turn out to be if she *were* alive, hiding somewhere, was not beyond what their relationship had taken her to, but, when the body was found, he wasn't surprised, only relieved. The parents must have felt the same sort of relief, he supposed, like the deliciously painful release of air you experience after swimming under water.

"She was a very good swimmer," Valerie's father said. He was a tall, angular sort of man, a retired air force pilot, with pilot's clear, narrow eyes. There was a tone of accusation in his voice.

"Yes, she was," Brad said.

"She won medals in high school."

"I know."

"She must have gotten a cramp," the woman said. She had a sad, tired, whiney sound. Brad realized they weren't really talking to him at all. For three days, since the moment they'd gotten the telephone call, or however the Mounties let people know about things like that, they'd been having this dialogue, this angerless argument:

"She was a very good swimmer."

"She must have gotten a cramp."

How else, but for the second statement, could the first one and the reality of her death be reconciled?

"Yes," Brad said. He wanted to say, "I always told her not to go out so far," but thought better of it—it would sound, he was sure, as if he were trying to shift blame away from himself—then, abruptly, changed his mind and blurted it out.

Valerie's father nodded, his eyes clear as water. If there was nothing in her mother's face to link her to Valerie, the father's face was like a tombstone, with the words "here lies the ghost of the other me" chiseled into his cheeks. He was clearly the father of the girl Brad had known and loved, and Brad felt a thin jab of tenderness for the man. "She was a *strong* swimmer," he said, but the tone of accusation was already beginning to fade.

In some ways, this was the hardest part. He'd never met her parents before, knew very little about them except that—on the face of it—they had made Val's life miserable, appeared to be the cause of all the screwiness in her and had been, when all else failed, a final *reason* to use against him. He had no idea what they knew of him, if anything, whether he was being joined now as the man who'd loved their daughter, who shared with them that pain, or being interviewed as the last person to have seen her alive, the man whose fault it may have been.

He told them, as decently and elusively as he could, something about the way she'd been on the last weekend of her life, something

about how she'd spent the time, but he found himself thinking, as he had, increasingly, for the past three days, of what
he had done, afterwards.

He remembered thinking, at some point as he walked around
the quarry, that the shit was over, that he was free, and although
he'd swept that thought quickly away, he didn't like that he'd
had it, no matter how briefly. He remembered, curiously, how
hoarse his voice had become from calling her name over and
over, and the deliberateness with which he had dressed
himself—pants over the still damp trunks, shirt left unbuttoned,
no shoes—before going off to call for help. He remembered the
careful way he had edged the Healey down the dirt road, past
rocks and clutches of weed, until he'd turned onto the blacktop.
He'd paused there to steady his hands and thought there should
be a sign, NO TRESPASSING or NO SWIMMING, and that
probably they would put one up now. He'd driven fast then,
with a controlled recklessness, and screeched to a dusty halt
at the first house he came to, asking to use the phone. He
remembered feeling guilty—actually that—when he'd explained
to the middle-aged woman who answered the door what had
happened, and the knowing look on her face, as if she knew
what had actually happened. But what the hell *had* happened?
What was there to know? It was just as he said it was—she went
out too far, she had drowned, there wasn't anything he could
have done to prevent it, short of somehow willing the pieces
of the day to lay down differently than they had. But no one
can do that, can they? The coolness of the big wooden-floored
farmhouse made him feel faint as he listened to the ringing on
the other end of the line, waiting for the police to answer, and
he placed his palm to his chest and felt his heart pounding under
the hard bone. He remembered how sore his throat was, from
all the shouting of her name, as he talked into the phone, and
the glass of lemonade the woman brought to him—it was cool,
but it tasted foul in his mouth, polluted.

"Were there any last words?" the father asked, interrupting.

"Excuse me?" Brad was genuinely surprised.

"I don't mean last words, exactly, but—well, what were you

talking about, the two of you, before she went in the water that time? Sometimes—I know, from the war—people say things, something, before they die that later seems to have some meaning."

Brad sipped at his coffee, thinking hard. "I don't remember. We were just talking. She was happy we'd gone swimming. She was just chattering on about all sorts of things, you know how people talk when they're happy. There wasn't anything special."

"It's not important," the father said.

"No," the mother said. She looked sadder, more tired, every minute. Brad wondered if she really was Valerie's mother—a step-mother, perhaps. After a moment, she added, "We're sure you did everything you could."

"Yes," the father said. He allowed himself to almost smile.

Brad didn't say anything.

That night, he had no urge for the whiskey he'd been dousing himself in three nights running and found himself wandering through grassy paths of the campus until he wound up standing in the hallway outside his office, his hand on the knob. He hadn't meant to go there, didn't recall going there, in fact, but he went in and sat down immediately at the typewriter, as if with a purpose. There was a sheet of paper in the machine and he stared at the several lines of words typed neatly at the top. It was a quote from Kant, something he'd wanted to record for use in his thesis, but it had no meaning for him now, just words arranged in a straight line but leading nowhere. He read the sentence several times without comprehension, then tore the paper out of the typewriter and crumpled it. He rolled a fresh sheet into the machine and sat staring at it for a long time, his mind blank as the luminescent paper.

While he waited for a pot of tea to brew, he went down the hall to the bathroom. Washing his hands in the sink, he stared at his face in the mirror—a long, morose face, with tired eyes, tanned skin and the kind of chin people thought of as purposeful. He was twenty-three years old, a graduate student in philosophy with most of the research for his dissertation done, no job prospects that he knew of, with nothing of value but a 1963 Healey in need of rear end work; a good-looking, well-built young man with a charming smile (so women told him) and a brilliant mind (so professors told him) but with little else to recommend him. If he and Valerie had been married, he thought, he would be a widower. A twenty-three year-old widower still in school. He began to laugh at that thought and the laughter turned to sobbing suddenly as the numbness which had surrounded him since the moment he'd pulled himself from the quarry's stinking water cracked, like dry mud in the sunlight. "I did," he sobbed, "I did, I did."

He didn't wait for the tea, though he did pause at his office long enough to unplug the electric kettle. He walked straight home then, to where the Healey sat parked under a streetlight, sleek and glistening, like a living thing, just asleep and waiting. He drove north out of town, carefully but fast, his hands tight on the leather-wrapped wheel. Lights were on in the farmhouse where he had used the telephone, and he thought of the anxious woman, his cheeks flushing. He wondered what she would say if he ever happened to meet her on the street—"Aren't you the young man who came to use the phone about that drowning? You said there was an accident, but you didn't say that when they found that poor girl she wouldn't have any clothes on"—and shame slipped into his mouth like saliva, leaving a bitter taste. He lit a cigarette to burn it away.

They had put a chain across the mouth of the dirt road, and a sign hung from it, its big red letters luminescent in the Healey's headlamps: NO TRESPASSING—NO SWIMMING. He doused the lights and parked on the side of the road, well out of the way of anyone passing by. Just out of the car, he went back and rummaged through the glove box till he found the old boy scout knife he kept for emergencies, wishing he had thought to bring something bigger. He studied the sign for a moment before slipping under the chain. "Huh," he snorted. The sound of his voice, sharp and loud in the wooded stillness, surprised him "Trespassers will be violated," he whispered.

It was a clear night, filled with specks of stars and an almost-full moon. It hung about him with the heavy prairie heat of August, sibilant with the sound of insects, damp with sweat.

The dirt trail beneath his feet was dark, the clumps of weed vague, wavering shadows, but the gravel heaps loomed like ghosts, grey and glistening, and beyond them the wrecked bridge hunkered down like some prehistoric beast feeding in the moonlight. The lime which had brought the quarrymen here a century earlier had left its mark on their deserted furniture and the clearing he walked through was stained with a pale glow, like the belly of a dead fish floating in shallow water.

He crossed the creaking bridge carefully, running his hand across the splintered beams, and then he was on the beach, rocks giving way suddenly to pebbles, then to sand. A bank of clouds rolled across the sky, blurring the moon and most of the stars. He sat down on a large rock and threw the stub of his cigarette into the black, almost invisible water. It went out with a hiss. The quarry pond extended before him like a black, hungry mouth with cleverly, cruelly hidden teeth. Frogs jumped boldly in the shallow water by his feet and mosquitos settled on his forearms to feed. A chorus of cicadas vibrated in the shadowed trees.

He took off his clothes and stood naked, with his feet in the water, the knife in his hands. The water was tepid, even now, and the slime oozed up around his toes. The frogs and waterbugs darted out of his way, and somewhere, way out in the blackness, there was a splash, as if something was preparing itself to meet him. He opened the blade of the knife and placed it between his teeth, biting hard on the cold, gritty steel. Then he began to wade, moving each foot carefully through the resistant water and muck which sought to pull him down. His toes sank into cold silt and strings of vegetation entwined themselves about his legs. When he was up to his knees, he dove in and began to swim.

He moved easily, almost silently through the darkness—taking long, smooth strokes, remembering the voices of the counsellors at the camp he'd gone to as a boy, shouting "breathe, stroke, breathe, stroke," over and over, gliding in the momentum—until he was tired. He was in water way above his head, far out into the spoon of the quarry itself, treading water quietly, breathing heavily, turning himself around in a tight circle. He couldn't see a thing.

Above him, the clouds shifted and stars peered through like bored patrons in opera boxes. The walls of the quarry rose around him, dark and silent, like tombstones, massive and pitiless. Somewhere, not too distant, there was a splash and the swift swish of some thing moving in the water. *There are no fish here*, Brad said to himself. *There is something out there. There is something in the water here with me.* There was a cold emptiness in a corner of his chest, and a slight pain around it, as if a section of his body had vanished and the muscles and organs and bones surrounding the vacancy were pressing in to see what had happened. He took the knife from his teeth and held it loosely in his right hand, opening and closing his fist around the handle. His jaws ached and his tongue retained the bitter taste of metal. *Come and get me*, he thought. Then he said it out loud, the sound of his cool, steady voice soothing him, like the sound of help arriving, in the distance. Then he shouted it: *Come and get me!*

He was thinking, at that very moment, of Valerie—for the first time in many hours during which he had, for the most part, thought only of himself. He was thinking of the smallness of her feet, and of the sweep of line formed by her body from the breast to the hip when she lay naked on her side in bed, and of her heavy eyes, so much like her father's, clear and narrow, seeing so much. But he couldn't remember their color.

For a long while there was silence, punctuated only by the soft splashing of the water around him as he bobbed in it. Even the cicadas had fallen silent. The swollen bank of clouds hovering above him was dissolving, and, looking up, Brad could see the stars as they appeared, in clusters. It seemed as if there were a million of them, and he smiled at that thought, because he knew there were, in fact, many millions, as many stars as there were moments of dread.

Slowly, like stars appearing through cloud, he opened his hand and let the knife fall from it, then, on an impulse, made a grab and retrieved it. He closed the blade, raised his arm above his head and threw the knife as far as he could into the darkness of the quarry, like a final offering. He heard it hit the water with a sharp plop and he fancied he could feel the ripples it formed.

Then he straightened himself out in the water and, slowly, pacing himself so as not to get too tired, but with firm, even strokes, he swam to shore. Behind him, in the darkness, the quarry was silent, like an eye closing in sleep.

AMONG STRANGERS

Snow was beginning to fall as they entered the freeway and Morton drove with exceptional care, as he always did when the weather was poor. At home, it had been raining, but it always seemed to rain in Brampton and he was used to it. The tires made a sharp hissing sound as they rolled through the slush, like a faint rebuke.

"Pick Abe to be born on a day like this," he said, his mouth puckering at the thought of his brother the way it did when he sucked the pulp from a slice of lemon in the dregs of his tea.

"*Morton*" Sarah said sharply. She was sitting up straight and as far from him as the broad solid seat of the Buick would allow, not because she didn't want to be near him, he knew, but because she liked to watch the countryside roll by, unfolding like one of those Chinese diaramas they had seen at the Royal Ontario. In airplanes, even when they were high above the clouds and there was really nothing to see, she kept her nose pressed to the window, oblivious to everything around her. Two winters before, when they'd driven to Florida on their vacation, she had actually gotten eyestrain. Morton had found it hard to believe but that was what the doctor they stopped in at in Atlanta said.

"How could Abe know it would snow on his birthday? Besides,

was it snowing the day he was born?'' She pivoted her head toward
him as she spoke, but her shoulders remained motionless, tilted
toward the window, and Morton marvelled, as he always did, at
the agility of her still graceful neck.

"Yes, as a matter of fact, it was."

"You can't remember that. You were only four."

"When you're four, you notice things like snow, believe me.
I'd gotten a new sled for *Chanukah*—actually, *Si* got a new sled
and I got his old one—and it hadn't snowed since. Not one lousy
flake. The day Abe was born, the skies opened up like they were
putting on a show to celebrate the blessed event, big, wet, fluffy
snowflakes, like today, and I was dying to try out the sled but
we had to go to the hospital with Poppa. A little trifling thing
like the birth of a brother spoiled my whole day. Sure I remember.
I hated him for it."

"Oh, Morton, you *didn't*. Do you really remember that?"

"Sure I do." He grinned, savoring the brief flash of heat he
felt toward his brother, though whether it was memory or
something closer he didn't know.

"A fine way to talk about your own brother," Sarah scolded
"and on his birthday. Besides, I don't believe you, you're making
it up."

"You're right," Morton said, raising his right hand from the
steering wheel in a gesture that could have been of futility or exas-
peration. They had just passed Hornby and there was still a long
way to go. "I'm making it up."

Sarah shook her head slowly and made a little sound, then let
her eyes swing gratefully back to the window, where a safe,
understandable world swept by with the same smooth motion as
an unwinding film at the movies.

"I wonder how those studded tires are?" Morton said after a
few minutes. Tires were a preoccupation of his since he'd had a
blowout on the Spadina with the other car and was lucky enough
only to have crumpled into the median. He lit a cigar and turned
on the vents. The heater was blasting away and it was stuffy in
the Buick.

They stopped in Woodstock for coffee, then headed back west

through the silently falling snow. They passed a sign saying *London, 50 kilometres*, and a snowplow with a revolving blue light. There wasn't much traffic.

"Are we going to Abe's first or directly to the home?" Sarah asked.

"The *home*. You call that a home? It's a half-way house, half-way to the cemetery. Yeh, we're going right there."

"Morton, you're not going to start that all over again, are you?"

He didn't answer.

"Morton, promise me, please."

"I won't start anything," he said grudgingly.

"I think sometimes you enjoy fighting with your brothers."

"Believe me, I don't enjoy it. I enjoy it about as much as Momma enjoys living in that *home*."

"You don't think she's happy there? It's a wonderful place, they've got all the medical services and religious facilities you could ask for, and..."

"Yes, and nice companionship," Morton interrupted, "and the food is good. Please, Sarah, don't start the litany of virtues of that place. I've heard them all a hundred times, from Abe and Si and Myrna and Rose. Don't let me hear them from you. And, anyway, I agree, God forgive me. I agree, it's a wonderful place. You couldn't ask for a better place to be put out to die in. With the Eskimos, there were probably some ice floes that were more desirable than others. That doesn't change it. Yeh, I'm sure Momma likes it there, better than some other places we might have sent her to. She has things to do, she can see old friends, the few that are left, and make some new ones, like just what she needs is new friends, right? And they take good care of her. I don't dispute that. But does all that, every one of those wonderful things, does that take away the hurt? Does all that erase the fact that her children don't want her?"

The only sound in the car was the faint hiss of the heater. Outside, he could hear the steady drone of the tires in the slush, like a distant wail, and the rhythmical clicking of the windshield wipers effortlessly doing battle with snow.

"You're being melodramatic," Sarah said finally. He could tell she had thought carefully before replying. "Like always," she added, forcing a smile.

"No, you're being over-realistic. Because a woman is in her eighties, she has to be senile. All right, maybe Momma *is* senile, I grant that. Does that mean she's devoid of feelings?"

"The doctors said...."

"I know, I know what the doctors said. She doesn't know half the time where she is anyway. She wouldn't *care* where she was. She's *happier*. Bull! I'm no professor of psychology but I don't buy all that bunk. Doctors tell you what they think you want to hear. Abe wants to hear that. Boy, oh boy, does he. But even if it was true what they say, does that change the fact that Abe got tired of taking care of her?"

There wasn't any answer to that so she offered none.

"If only she'd come to stay with us," she said softly.

"You don't believe that stuff Abe dreamed up about her not wanting to leave London, do you?"

"She *has* lived there most of her life, Morton. And she does have a lot of nice friends there. And she said it herself."

"Bah. There's a hole you could drive this Buick through in all those arguments. If she doesn't know where she is half the time, like they say, it wouldn't kill her to leave London. And the half of the time she did know where she was, she'd know she was with her son and daughter-in-law who love her at least. Friends? Most of them are dead, or in homes, too, and they don't go around visiting. And as for her saying so, well, Abe said so, so she said so." He lifted his hands from the wheel for a second to make a gesture of annoyed futility. The car didn't waver, the tires slicing through snow like a sleigh propelled by an invisible team of horses.

"No, Abe wouldn't permit that. He's the favorite, and after she lives with him all those years, for me to take her in then would only make it obvious, even to her, that he was kicking her out. Even to her. No, she has to go to the home to get him off the hook, big shot Abe, so everybody thinks he's doing her a big favor parting with her, giving this golden opportunity to die among strangers."

He almost missed the exit for London and the car swerved badly, giving them a scare. The old age home was on the other side of the city and he drove slowly through the snow-clogged streets. He parked in the lot as close to the building as possible and checked his watch.

"Half an hour late."

They saw Abe's station wagon parked nearby but neither could remember what Si was driving the last time they'd seen him. They shook the dusting of snow from their coats at the door. Morton had a box of chocolates for his mother under one arm, a box of cigars for his brother under the other.

"Here they are," a voice called as the heat from the vestibule attacked their faces. "And about time. You took a bus?"

Abe was coming toward them, hand extended, face gleaming. Morton shook his brother's hand, slipping an arm around his shoulder. "Happy birthday, Abe. You look pretty good for your age, I must admit. What is it? Fifty?"

"*Fifty?* You mean you're admitting to being fifty-four? I'm saying forty-six and I've got a driver's license to prove it. And a mother to back me up. She was there at the great occasion."

They had moved across the wide room and were in the centre of the cluster of people around the old woman. Sarah was kissing Myrna and Rose. Morton shook hands with Si quickly, then knelt beside his mother.

"Momma? It's Morton. Look, I brought you chocolates, with the cherries? Your favorite."

"Morton?" Her voice was thin as water, like her body, like her fingers clutching at the box, like her transparent hair.

"Oh, I gave you the wrong box. Here. This one is for Abe. For his birthday." He rose, a pain shooting from his knees to his chest. "Abe? Here, for you. *Mazeltov*. And many happy returns."

"Cigars? You always give me cigars. You have no imagination, Morty."

"I admit it. What can you get for a man who has everything? I thought about a sled but Sarah said no."

"A sled?"

"Sure, I had a nice red one in mind."

"*Morton*," Sarah said behind him.

"So, tell me, Myrna," Morton said quickly, "what did *you* give your darling husband on his natal anniversary?"

Myrna giggled. "*Morton*, you dirty old man. That sounds positively, deliciously obscene." She took her husband's arm. "You know this new series of Beethoven they're doing? Seventy-five records? I won't even tell you how much it costs."

"I was reading about it in *The Globe*," Morton said. "They're not all out yet, I understand."

"I had to order them. All he really got was a card announcing it."

"A gyp," Si said morosely.

"I didn't know you liked Beethoven," Morton said.

"Like him? I never heard of him before today."

"So, Morton, you look good," Si said. "How's the law treating you? Okay?"

"Sure, I can't complain. And you? How's business, as they say?"

"Like you. I can't complain. You know how it goes, business is business. The economy of the country, though, *oiy*. That Trudeau, he should have his head examined."

"Or better yet, chopped off," Abe said. "*Then* examined."

"Did you hear about Abe's promotion?" Myrna asked, beaming.

"Another promotion? Oh, that's wonderful," Rose squealed.

"How could there be another promotion?" Morton asked. "You already have the whole province, don't you?"

"So now I have Quebec, too," Abe said, shrugging. "And the Maritimes, whatever the hell they are. No big deal. So, come on, already, let's go celebrate. It's my birthday and I'm the whole eastern Canada district manager, starting Monday. So let's go eat. It's on me."

Morton took his mother's arm and helped her up. He could tell she recognized him, that she was happy. He wondered if she *could* understand what was going on around her, what was being said. There was a blank, faraway look in her eyes and her hand

trembled on his arm, but she was smiling. She looked weaker
than last time, weaker and thinner and paler. She wore a fur
coat Abe had given her three years before and wobbly-heeled
shoes and a black hat. He could hear the clicking of the heels
as they walked slowly to the door.

"How are you feeling, Momma? They treating you all right
here? Everything all right? You sure you wouldn't like to come
home with Sarah and me tonight, just for a little while?" Morton was whispering, like a conspirator. "Just to see how you
like it?"

She didn't answer and Morton didn't pause between his questions. He didn't expect an answer. It was hard to think of things
to say.

"You stay here out of the snow and I'll bring the car around,"
Abe said. He had slipped into his overcoat but was hatless.
Morton watched him descend the steps and cross the parking
lot. The snow was still falling and it was beginning to get dark.

"Maybe we should stay for the night," he said to Sarah. "I
don't like to drive through this kind of stuff in the dark."

"Why don't you?" Myrna asked. "Si and Rose are staying
over but we've got plenty of room. The children are both away
and their rooms are just gathering dust."

That stung, the image of the hollow rooms flashing into
Morton's mind as his mother's bony arm shifted uneasily in
his grip, but he had promised Sarah, and he gave her a fleeting
glance before he answered. "You want us to stay in a dusty
room?" he asked, laughing.

"Wouldn't catch me driving on a night like this," Si said.

"Friday," the old woman said suddenly.

Her voice was so thin, so ragged, the sound of it impressed
Morton more than the meaning of the solitary word. He
squeezed her arm gently.

"We're going to a nice restaurant, Momma. It's Abe's birthday and he just got a wonderful new job. We're going to
celebrate. All of us, Si and Rose and Abe and Myrna and Sarah
and me and you." He smiled into the faces of his brother and
sisters-in-law to show his inclusion of them was genuine.

"Friday," the old woman said again, and her thin lips tightened, her eyes narrowed. There was a faint glaze over her eyes, as if a drop of milk had been squeezed onto each pupil. "No ride."

"Oh, God," Morton said. "Of course, it's Friday. Si, is there a restaurant we can walk to?"

"Around here? I don't know, we can ask Abe. Here...."

The station wagon had pulled up in front of the steps and the blare of the horn drowned out Si's words. Morton could see his younger bother wiping at the frost on the inside of his windshield.

"Wait here." He steered his mother to Sarah's hand and opened the door. A blast of icy air caught him by surprise and he raised his collar as he negotiated the slick stairs.

Abe rolled his window down. "What's holding things up?"

"Abe, for God's sake, it's Friday."

"So?"

"You know Momma won't ride on Friday after dark. You know she can't."

"Ah, that's nonsense. Come on...."

"Abe, she's never ridden on Friday after sunset or on Saturday, you know that, just like she's never missed *shul* on Saturday or services Friday night. You know she...."

"She doesn't know what day it is, for Chrissake," Abe said, opening his door.

"She knows, she knows. *I* didn't think of it—she told me."

"Ah, crap," Abe said.

"Isn't there someplace we can walk to?"

"There's no place around for blocks. Besides, she can't walk far, you know that. Why the hell didn't you get here on time, it'd still be light and she wouldn't be worrying her head with this crap, she'd be enjoying herself."

Morton felt the blood rise in his face and he clenched his bare hands into painful, numbing fists. "You think it wouldn't have gotten dark?" he spit out. "Come on, we can eat here. They have a cafeteria. We can...."

"Are you crazy? Morty? Are you crazy?" Abe swung out of the car. "Come on, we'll settle this."

"*Abe.*" The wind tore the word out of his mouth and he

followed his brother's shoulders up the steps.

"Momma, what's this?" Abe was smiling, stroking her face with one gloveless hand. "What's this? Tell *Abela*."

"Friday," the old woman whispered. The sound she made was like the crackling of dry leaves and it sent the pain shooting through Morton's chest again, making him wince.

"No, no, Momma. It's not Friday, it's Thursday. Yesterday was Wednesday, *tomorrow* is Friday."

"Friday," she repeated, but there was a shade of uncertainty in her cracked voice.

"No, no, Momma. Honestly, it's Thursday. Come on, now, we're going to a nice restaurant, we're going to celebrate my birthday. Remember, Momma , the pain I caused you forty-six years ago? Or maybe it was forty-seven?" He looked up at Morton and winked. "You always said I was the hardest. Today, I'll make it up to you."

"Friday?" she said again, but this time it was more a question.

"No, Momma. *Thursday. Tomorrow* is Friday. We'll go to *shul* together in the evening, you and I. It's Thursday, isn't it, Myrna?"

His wife nodded her head slowly.

"Myrna?"

"*Yes.*"

"Si, isn't it Thursday?"

Si shrugged. He was the eldest, and had taken off on his own the earliest. "Sure, sure, Thursday, Wednesday, what difference does it make? Yes, Momma, it's Thursday." He leaned forward, nodding his face close to hers. There was a shaving nick on his cheek.

"See? I told you, Momma. Morton? Isn't it Thursday?"

Morton turned his face away. "Yes," he said softly, ashamed. "It's Thursday."

"See, Momma," Abe said, "even the lawyer says so, so it must be so. It's not Friday. You were just a little confused, that's all, no big deal. Ah, it must be nice to lead a life of leisure, you don't even have to keep track of the days." He winked at his brothers. "With me, it's minute by minute. Hey, *Mommela*, would we lie to you? would *I* lie to you?"

They went out into the cold. Morton took one of his mother's arms, Sarah the other. They looked at each other over the old woman's head but didn't say anything.

It was colder than he had thought it ever could be. The snow was falling heavier, muffling the ground beneath it. It would be a long drive home through the snow.

ON AN APRIL MORNING

The sun rose that morning with all the same certainty that we have always known it to. A slow greying first, as if the cloth of blackness were breathing, the fibres coming loose; then a pulsing streak of something more than grey but less than light; and then light itself, a breaking up of all else there had been, a chasing of shadows, a lifting, a softening, again. Hop sat on the stone step of the porch he had built during the first summer of their marriage and observed all of this with the simple consciousness of what was happening, but no more; his eyes strayed occasionally from his fisted hands, hanging as if by a life and will of their own, disconnected, between his thighs, to the beginning morning hovering so cautiously over the fields as if entangled in the crowns of the erect pines on the horizon. It seemed to him he had been sitting like that forever; a long while ago, he remembered, a stiffness had crept through his crumpled body and a chillness had sprung from the marrow of his bones, but he felt nothing now and he couldn't recall when his consciousness of irritation and discomfort bordering on pain had ceased. It was funny, he thought, the way the muscles' vitality and elasticity gives way to arthritis and pain, but then to numbness, an absence of all sensation, more like in a circle than a straight line, the way he'd always thought life took us. His wide flat brow read with the rippled braille of sweat; the brilliant aluminum glint of his eyes had tarnished to the smooth dull blare of iron. Pretty soon, he thought, I'll get up. It's morning and I guess I'm hungry. Sara will fix breakfast, no, Lois will fix breakfast, and then we'll have to get to work. The plowing, and those gullies in the far field to be filled, and that piece in the big barn. All that today. Gotta do that soon. Especially the barn work, before we get too busy in the fields. Damn, I guess I sure shoulda done it last week—hell, last month, when there wasn't nothin else to do anyways. Sara told me I should but I guess I didn't. His fingers, long and coated with a thick layering of dead polished skin, swung almost lazily, brushing against the cuffs of his overalls and the elastic tops of his red and brown socks. Lastic comin loose. Sara'll have to buy me some new ones soon, all of them gettin this way, or do somethin to fix em. I mean Lois. Lois'll have to. His stubbled cheeks hollowed with the motion of his tongue as he licked the edges of his teeth, and colored with the rising warmth that had begun to spread through his limbs and the thin blue veins of his skin. A horse whinnied somewhere and the stamping of restless cowsfeet mingled with the tentative clucking of chickens in the grey light sifting through the yard. In the kitchen behind him, the clattering of pans, the striking of a match, the silent wiping of hands on whispering starched cloth, and the mute laughter of heels and toes on the linoleumed floor formed the fragile wall of sound to which his back was turned.

"Pop?" The question was like a silver bell calling him back from wherever he had been. "Pop? Is that you sittin out there?" Lois stood framed in the wiregauze doorway touching the coiled spring gingerly with her fingertips. He turned his head wearily but all he could see was the grey form of her behind the cross-ings of the screen. In the early stamping stillness her voice had sounded strangely like Sara's. Funny that he hadn't noticed that before. "That you, Lois?" he asked the doorway, just to be sure.

"Yes, Pop," she answered, pulling at the spring, letting it go, listening to the strength of its coil. "You been out there all night, Pop? Didn't you *ever* go to bed?" Her words punctured the day like shining knives and sunk, soundlessly, into the ground at his feet, leaving a terrible void. She fidgeted with her apron. Pop, are you all right? she wondered. The pockets of her eyes felt tight and damp and worried. After awhile, the force of her eyes on his back pushed him up and he wiped the seat of his faded blue jumper with his rough palms. His red flannel shirt was open beneath the jumper's straps and Lois could see the first beads of sweat glinting on the thick mat of curling hair on his chest.

"I guess so," he said. "I guess I just forgot." He moved slowly up the stone stairs and scraped his heavy leather shoes by habit on the top step before moving onto the porch itself and across to the door. Through the screen, he could see Lois's smooth tight face, like a younger Sara. "Your mother up yet?" he asked her through the screen. Her face, although only inches away from his, was sufficiently obscured by the tight wire mesh that the sudden spasm which traveled the breadth of her cheek went unnoticed. "Pop?" she asked, a shining knife. "Are you all right? Mommy's dead. Don't you remember? Pop?" The knives cut him and left him bloodless, standing there. "Yeah, that's right," he said. "I guess I forgot." Sara dead? I guess I forgot.

He opened the door and walked past her into the kitchen. She followed and the tight coiled spring swung the door closed with a hollow sloppy bang.

He drank a cup of coffee while Lois was frying the eggs. He sat at the red enamel-topped table with his hairy arms bare and sweating in front of him, the palms upward on either side of his plate. The coffee cup steamed under his nose and he breathed heavily until the dry hairs of his nostrils were wet and warm and clinging. Coffee smells like Sara's mouth. Sara's tongue tastes like coffee and sugar and cream. Like thick sweet coffee.

Lois bustled over the frying pan, annoying the eggs with nervous thrusts of a spatula. Harry came swinging down the stairs whistling, as if he had forgotten too; he silenced himself abruptly as he came into the kitchen, remembering quickly. He stood in the doorway scanning the room but saying nothing until his sister looked up and caught his glance, then he walked briskly to her side. "Is he all right?" he whispered.

"I don't know," Lois answered, anxiously watching the eggs. "He's actin queer. He don't say hardly nothin. Except, he asked me if she were up yet. I mean, like he forgot she was dead at all but just upstairs still asleep. Like nothin had happened at all. But then I reminded him and he just said oh, yeah, I forgot, and that was all. He don't say hardly nothin." Her eyes went from Harry's to her father sitting motionlessly at the table and back to Harry again. "Do you think we should call Bobby again? I mean, do you think we might have to?"

Harry stared down at his hands for a moment and then put them gently on Lois's. The four hands, locked in one spot with the handle of the spatula awkwardly caught between them, trembled slightly, but he couldn't tell which one of them was causing it. He himself had since forgotten to be conscious of any fear that might exist within him, although he knew one did, at least one. "He'll be all right," Harry said. "We'll take care of him. Don't worry." He smiled awkwardly and Lois took her hands away and turned back to the stove. "Pop," Harry said, in his full clear voice, "good mornin, Pop," and sat down at the table beside his father.

"Good mornin, Harry," Hop answered, hardly moving. "Up already, are you?" It was an odd thing to say, Harry thought, squinting, since he was always up at this time, sometimes earlier. "That's good," Hop went on, "we've got a busy mornin, a busy day to take care of. We've got all that plowin to get started on and those gullies have gotta be filled in. And I've gotta get that piece of roof in the big barn fixed before we get too thick into the plowin. Shoulda done the foolish thing last week like your mother said we should." He stared into his coffee and then looked up again at Harry, at Harry's eyes, Sara's eyes, really, in Harry's craggy face.

Lois was filling plates on the counter, clucking with her tongue. "And another thing," Hop said abruptly, looking away from Harry's eyes, "we've got to go into town today too. Maybe be best to do that first off, get it over with, right after eatin." He moved his cup and saucer to make room for the steaming plate of yellow and white and crisp brown Lois was dangling in front of him. "To town?" Harry leaned forward, asked. "To get your mother," Hop said quietly. Lois swallowed once, hard, and stared through the brightening screen of the door and clenched her fists tightly in the small pockets of her white starched apron.

The silence of their breakfast was broken only by the clicking of the suction caused by tongues kissing teeth and the sliding whirr of chewing. A grey terrier came to the kitchen door and scratched at the screen. "Bozo's here," Lois said, as if making an announcement of some importance, and she got up from the table to let him in. Hop stared at the dog silently and then offered him a scrap of bread dripping with yolk. The dog licked lazily at his hand, devoured the bread in one gulp, and curled at his feet, whining. "I believe Bozo misses your mother," Hop said. Lois, sitting again, sucked at her coffee cup. It was the first thing he'd said this day that made sense. "More coffee, Pop? Harry?" She jumped to her feet. "No, thank you, dear," Hop said, rising. Harry shook his head nervously. "You just about ready now, son? I'd like to get goin."

"To town?" Harry said.

Hop fingered one strap of his jumper idly and stared through the screen. He opened the door and walked out onto the porch, stopping the door from slamming with the heel of his shoe. He stood staring silently at the yard, his knees locked, head erect, arms loose at his sides. His eyes were dark and hollow.

Harry rose slowly from the table, pushing the chair back with the tender skin of the curve of his leg below the knee. "Jesus," he said.

Lois bit her lip and made her little fists. "He's goin to bring her home just like he said he would," she said. "He's goin to bring her home. We should have known that just because they said he couldn't, he wouldn't do it. We should have known. He's stubborn. I'll call Bobby. I'll call him now." She moved quickly across the kitchen to the wall phone above the counter.

"Don't," Harry said. "Don't bother. We'll go into town and we'll see Bobby at the funeral place. He said he'd be there this

mornin, seein to things. Don't worry. Bobby'll talk to him and
it'll be all right. He raised his hand slowly until his vision of her
was obstructed by the shape of his fingers, rounded to form an
O. "I'll call from town. You stay in the house and wait. Don't
worry." He took a cap from the sideboard and planted it firmly
on his head. "Really," he said, and went outside to join his father.

Hop was standing on the lowest step watching the dust beginning to rise in the heat of the yard. He didn't move at all until
Harry was standing beside him, then he merely lowered his head.

"The truck or the Buick?" Harry asked.

"Get the team," Hop said.

"The team? The horses?"

"Bring em to the old barn."

"The old barn?" Harry said. "We're taking the buckboard?"
His voice was like a spray of pebbles in his father's face. "Yes,"
Hop said, and shrugged his shoulders and moved off tiredly toward
the barns. Sara's old buckboard, we came here first in it, we'll
come home in it now. He walked slowly through the dust.

Harry stopped the team behind Bobby's pickup truck with a
sigh of relief to see it there, rusted and mud-spattered and still
giving off the faint tingle of sound motion imparts to machinery
even after they're still, and wrapped the leather strands twice
around the brake handle. The horses stamped their feet on the
unaccustomed pavement and lowered their heads, flicking their
ears, rubbing their noses gingerly against the strange ground.
"Looks like Bobby's here too," Harry said hopefully. His father
said nothing but nodded in agreement, then swung his legs easily
around to the side and dropped heavily to his feet on the sidewalk.
"Do you guess it's all right to leave the team here alone?" Harry
asked, getting down on his side. "I don't see why not," Hop said.
"We'll just be inside."

The sun was rising steadily, leaving a burning trail in its wake.
Hop's skin seemed to be bathed in sweat and his flannel shirt
clung heavily to his back and under his arms. The loose folds
of his pant legs brushed quietly against each other as he walked
to the door, upon which, in gilt letters, was inscribed the words

BROWN'S CHAPEL MORTUARY, and opened it. Behind him, chafing on the sidewalk like the horses, Harry followed.

"Mr. Hopwood," Brown said.

"Hop," said Bobby Goodnight. "Harry. Warm day. I see you're drivin your buckboard. How do those horses like the town, Harry?"

Hop didn't smile to them or say anything at all. He looked around the room, observed the black and red drapes, the thick rusty carpet, the cold brown tables, the full rusty leather chairs. Then he looked at the two men, the one sweating and impatient in his faded denims and dusty boots, his brother-in-law, and friend, and the other cool and plump in his tight black suit, his face as bland as a husk of wheat, a stranger, practically, who waited upon him. "Is she ready?" he said, quickly, finally.

"The funeral will be tomorrow, as we've planned, if that's all right with you, Mr. Hopwood," Brown said, rubbing the round roll of his belly with the bottoms of his soft white hands.

"I'll take her with me now," Hop said, looking at no one, "if she's ready."

"She's....your wife is ready, sir, I mean prepared, yes, Mr. Hopwood, but, as you know, the funeral has been planned for tomorrow, as we *all* agreed to yesterday, and we can't just change our plans right in the middle like that. Now, if you'll just leave everything to me, I'm sure everything will be fine and I'm sure that you'll have no reasons for dissatisfaction." Brown's blond face sweated slightly, with a nervous smiling. "I know exactly what you want, no pomp, no words, just a simple, old-fashioned burial. I can understand that, we get all sorts of reactions, all sorts of requests in this business, you know." He smiled again, this time with sympathy.

"Old-fashioned nothin," Hop said. He made huge hairy fists out of his lifeless hands and pressed them against his thighs. "Old-fashioned, that's somebody else's business, not mine. My only business is her. No pomp, no words, huh, that's nothin. That's nothin to do with it. You understand, huh. You understand nothin. Plans hell, let me have the coffin and I'll pay you, thank you very much, and goodbye. That's all. Nothin else. Nothin."

Hop stood with his feet spread wide apart and his muddy brown work shoes pressed deeply into the carpet's soft, rich plush, his legs like girded spans of a bridge tight within the loose folds of pants draped almost serenely around them, his fisted hands twisted on his hips, gently pressing against the bone. He looked at Brown and felt nothing; he looked at Bobby and felt nothing; he could sense Harry behind him, but he felt nothing. He could feel Sara in the room; Sara, whose tongue is like coffee and rolls on rainy mornings; Sara, whose tongue is rotting in her mouth.

Like a fist, hard yet flexible, like a pair of eyes, darkened and dry and on the verge of moisture, Hop loosened; like a fist unclenching, muscles coming out of a spasm, eyes gently closing, his face drawn, the skin about his eyes and lips lax and dark with the great hard void beneath and beyond and all but gone, he opened his hands, raised one, gingerly touched the buckle of his jumper.

"I've got a wagon, Bobby," he said. "I'd like to take her home in that. Would you help us out with her? I'd appreciate it." He looked at Bobby and flicked his hands up and out, gently, softly. Behind him, Harry, suddenly remembering, took off his cap.

Brown looked to Bobby in desperation, his thick eyelids fluttering. Bobby chewed his lower lip, looked, once, hastily around the room, as if for support, and then walked forward, slowly, taking his brother-in-law by the arm. "Listen, Hop," he said, "we talked about this yesterday. You remember that. Jesus, you know I'd like her to be buried on the farm as much as you would. I'm her brother. I haven't forgotten. I loved her too."

"I'm her husband," Hop said.

"I know that, Hop. I know. But I knew her too. I remember her saying how much she wanted to be buried on the farm, she said that lots of times. Shit, before she married you, even when we was still kids, she always used to say she wanted to be buried on Dad's farm. She had a special field picked out, too, and a place where she wanted the grave to be. A little hill under a goddamn willow." Bobby's voice was thick. He stared at the rusty plush which his feet seemed to sink into. "Under a goddamn willow. Jesus, what a spooky girl that sister of mine was, eh? Even as a kid she used to talk about that. But all right, what I mean to say is she always said that, and then when she married you it was the same thing, except that instead of Dad's farm it was yours where she had a place picked out."

"So why're we arguing?" Hop said.

"So she wanted to be buried on your farm; you want to do it, I want to do it; Mr. Brown here would be happy to do it; we all want to do it, for God's sake. But that doesn't change the law, Hop."

"It's not my law," Hop said. "I never knew it till yesterday. I never heard about it, never voted it, never needed it. It's not my law. It's not doin me any good and I'll be damned if I'll let it do me any bad. Now I'm goin to do it, Bobby Goodnight, and I'd be obliged if you'd help, but I'll do it without you, too."

He backed away from Bobby's hand and went around him. "Mr. Brown, if you'll just show me and my boy to where the box is, we'll be takin it and goin. You'll send me a bill and I'll pay it, you don't have to worry none about that."

"It's not that," Brown said. "I don't know. You know this is against the law. I mean, nowadays people just get buried in cemeteries or get cremated and that's all there is to it."

"That ain't all there is to it," Hop said back to him. "She ain't just people. She's my wife. And it's my concern, not any of yours."

"Yes, I know that, surely, and I respect your wishes, surely, too, if you're trying to carry out some last wish of hers or something......"

"Oh, God, don't I have better things to do than talk to you all day?" Hop said. "Listen, I don't know why they make a foolish law like that. I'm sure they didn't have me in mind special when they did make it, but I guess they didn't have me in mind at all or they wouldn't have made it at all either. I don't care if it's a zoning law or a health law or whatever kind of damn law it is, there's some other laws, there's some people laws that come first. And this is a people law. That's all."

Brown hemmed, and hedged. He was a citizen too. "Yes, well, that's true, Mr. Hopwood, but still, a law's a law, and you can get into a little trouble here and...."

"I guess I can give a little trouble too, to anybody who maybe gives me a little trouble," Hop said. He smiled, almost, but only for a moment. Oh, Jesus, this ain't the way I want it, Sara, not this, just you to take away again. Not this, Sara.

"Come on," he said quietly. "Just show us where she is and we won't bother you anymore. I hired you to get her ready, that's all, not to bury her. If there's law broken, it's me doin it, not you."

Brown crumbled. "All right. All right. Come this way." He shrugged, lifting his hands in a gesture of compliance, and looked disapprovingly in Bobby's direction. "You're my witness, Mr. Goodnight, that I did everything I could."

"Yes, you did," Bobby said.

Brown led the way to the rear of the room and through heavy, rust-colored drapes which covered, Hop saw as he followed, only darkness.

Sara, Sara whose tongue is like coffee and rolls in the early morning, Sara who is dead, are you dead, dear Sara, are you really dead?

They were in the wagon, he and Harry and Bobby, who had left his truck in front of the funeral place, as if to rot there, and the box which he could hardly believe could hold Sara, even if only just her body, it was so small and she had been so big, to him, so big, once, in the back, and it was afternoon already, more than half the day gone and so little done, so much more to do. There was a sun in the sky, high, and it danced on the back of his neck and drew the sweat from his skin like a rod bringing water up out of the ground.

Sara, Sara, are you in that box? Are you in there, oh, God, are you in there while I'm out here? Oh, Jesus, Sara, I didn't want it like that today, I swear to you, with fighting almost, I just wanted to take you out of there and take you away and take you home and put you in our ground. Like I promised, like I'm doing. I didn't want it like that but it's all right now. It's all right now, we're almost home, it's all right now. But that box, Jesus, are you really in that box, Sara, that little box? I guess it's big enough, but it looks so small for you, you were so big, so small really, but so big with me, so big when I looked at you or touched you. Oh Jesus, Sara. Oh God. Oh Sara, are you really in there, are you really dead? Sara? Are you really gone?

Harry brushed a fly away from his face. Bobby brushed at his face too, but there were no flies there. The horses trotted slowly home. They stopped in front of the house and Lois came out, wiping her hands on her apron wrinkled from the day but just as white as it had been in the morning. From where she stood on the porch, she could see the coffin in the back of the wagon, the old buckboard she and Harry had gone for rides in when they were children. "You brought her," she said. Then she began to cry. They sat in the wagon watching her come down the stone steps that he had settled there that first summer of their marriage, a long while ago, and come up to it and put her hands on the side boards and let the tears come running crazily down her cheeks and creep into the hollows of her nostrils. "Mommy," she sobbed. "Mommy, mommy, mommy."

"Get in," Hop said.

Then the horses went up into the field, pulling that wagon, until they came up to that tree and it wasn't a willow but it was a cotton-wood and it was weeping too, and they stopped under it. They all got out and they lowered the coffin down to the ground and he brought out the shovels and they began to dig. He stood in the broken earth swinging his shovel until his whole being was saturated with sweat. Bobby and Harry tired and they stood on the edge of the deepening hole with Lois and watched him while he went on digging. This was his field, his land, his and hers too once, now, always. Lois, standing on the rim with her little fists tight in her apron pockets, crying, it wasn't her land. Harry, behind her, cap tilted, face drawn, with her eyes, Sara's, unsee-ing in his head, it wasn't his land either, not really his. Bobby, beside them, red wild hair like a flag flapping in the slight breeze, it wasn't his. But he, in that hole of land, his arms straining, shirt clinging to his skin, shoes filled with the land, the hollows of his eyes filled with the dust of that land and drying unshed tears, was part of it, as was she, Sara, whose tongue is like honey and tea. Sara whose mouth is like coffee and cream and sugar. Sara.

And behind him, the sun was setting. The sun, it was setting; the sun, good God, was setting.

THE CALLER

Lewis was reading when the telephone rang and he hung on tenaciously to the sentence he was following, letting it pull him to the end of the paragraph before he grudgingly rose on the fourth ring. Judy was taking a shower and there was no one else but him to go. He spent a good part of his working day on the telephone and in the evening, at home, he hated to be drawn to the damn machine.

As he walked into the kitchen, and even as he was picking up the receiver, he was wondering who could be calling. They had only been in the house for two weeks, in the city one week more, and they had no friends yet, knew hardly anyone besides the people in his office. He couldn't remember a call yet on their slick yellow wall phone that hadn't been a wrong number. "Yes?" he said.

There was a silence for a moment on the other end of the line, a hesitation he knew the sound of his voice must have triggered, and he knew the call was a wrong number. Then a tiny, fuzzy voice whispered, "Is my mother there?"

It was a child's voice, whether boy or girl he couldn't tell. It sounded choked, distant, furtive, perhaps frightened. Lewis smiled warily. "No, honey, she isn't. I think you have the wrong number. Did you dial carefully?"

There was another hesitation, then the quavering voice again: "Is my mother there?"

Without meaning to, Lewis became impatient. "I'm sorry, honey, you have the wrong number. Dial again more carefully this time." He started to hang up but the voice pulled him back to the receiver, urgent this time, immediate. "Isn't this 624-1736?"

That *was* the number and Lewis was surprised to hear it, glanced at the phone just to make certain. "Yes," he started to say, but the voice cut him off: "Mrs. Andrews said my mother was there. Let me talk to her."

He was exasperated now; without reason, almost angry. "Listen, son," he said, sure now that his caller was a boy, "your mother isn't here....."

"You're a liar," the voice shouted and then the earpiece erupted into laughter. Then there was a click and the line went dead. Lewis hung up and stood for a moment staring at the phone before he shrugged and went back to the livingroom and his book. He found the paragraph he'd just finished and read it through again to get back into the action but found he couldn't get any farther. The call troubled him strangely, made him jittery and he got up from the couch to lock the front and rear doors.

The voice had sounded so much like that of a child, a little boy of perhaps five or six, frightened by something and wanting his mother, but he had acted so peculiarly. It was the accusation of lying, and that awful laugh, that had rattled him, Lewis knew. What a strange thing for a child to say, and what a strange laugh. And why the laugh at all, if the caller had indeed been a frightened child?

Perhaps it had been a child after all, he thought as he prowled around the house, listening to the fierce running of water in the bathroom, but not frightened, perhaps not as young as he had thought. A ten-year-old, calling numbers at random to amuse himself. Maybe even a teen-ager, killing time with a perverse joke. But the laugh, its memory still ringing in his ears, cold and unexpected, harsh and mirthless, nagged at him. A burglar, checking to see if anyone was home? An anonymous caller beginning a whole series of unsettling intrusions? Then again, he thought with some remorse, perhaps his caller had in fact been a child, a genuinely frightened child whose laugh and accusation was inspired by hysteria, and he chided himself guiltily for not having attempted to keep the boy talking, draw more out of him.

Lewis was not a timid man by nature, not a worrier especially, but he felt suddenly cold and vulnerable, as if someone were watching him from a dark corner of the house. He checked the doors again and made sure all the windows were locked and the curtains and drapes were drawn. He stood gazing through the kitchen window with comfort at the brightly shining porch light of a neighbor until he heard the shower turn off and he felt relieved a few minutes later when Judy came out of the bathroom, looking pink and fresh in her flowered bathrobe, a towel wrapped around her hair.

"Is that a great shower," she said, kissing him on the cheek. "It's such a luxury, I can't get enough of it. Never again will we live somewhere that doesn't have one."

She lit a cigarette and shook out her hair. "Who was on the phone?" she asked.

"Just a wrong number," Lewis shrugged. He went back to his book while she crawled into bed with a magazine. He felt better, as if having shrugged off the call to his wife he could now accept it that way himself. When he finished the chapter he was reading he took a shower and by the time he got into bed he'd forgotten the call.

Lewis was thirty-two, a native New Yorker and graduate of City College, a veteran of the pre-Vietnam Air Force. He worked as a public relations executive for a paper manufacturer and, after four years in the New York office, where he was one of many, had been transferred to San Francisco, where he was second man in the office, with a whole phalanx of "communications specialists" beneath him. The company he worked for, which grew thousands of acres of trees in the northwest, cut them down and ground them into pulp in order to make newsprint, napkins, writing paper and tissues, had become especially sensitive to the growing concern about the environment, and he had been put in charge of the counterattack against the critics. It was hard, stimulating work, involving the coming up with of ideas for campaigns and seeing to it that they were put into action. He had a good group of guys working with him and he was expecting a call from one of them three days after the night of his peculiar caller when the phone rang.

"I'll get it," he said, getting up from the table. They had just finished dinner and Judy was stacking the dishes in the washer while Lewis sipped at his second cup of coffee. "It's probably Stein."

He picked up the receiver and cradled it against his shoulder, reaching for a pad and pencil. "Hello? Stein?"

"Is my mother there?" a voice whispered and the memory of that laugh reverberated through Lewis's head. He snapped up straight, clenching the phone in his hand, his brow furrowing. Before he could say anything he realized how silly he was being and he relaxed, smiling, shaking his head at himself.

"Who is this?" Lewis asked gently.

"Bobby," the quavering little boy's voice said. "Can I speak to my mother?"

"Your mother isn't here, Bobby. You called here a few days ago, remember? You're dialing the wrong number. Now hang up and dial again, *carefully*."

There was a pause and Lewis smiled softly, picturing the puzzled frown on the boy's face. "Isn't this 624-1736?" the boy asked. He *did* sound puzzled, as if, somehow, he was being cheated by a force he couldn't understand, or a grown-up—just as bad.

Lewis glanced at the number on the phone, as he'd done the first time, just to reassure himself, and nodded. "Yes, it is, Bobby, but your mother isn't here. Whoever wrote down the number for you got it wrong. Probably just one of the numbers is wrong." He was feeling proud of himself now, for being so calm when his first reaction had been irritation, and for being so reasonable and helpful to what was obviously just a little boy trying to call his mother. "Is there anybody there you can ask about the number?"

There was another confused pause, then the boy asked,

demanded really: "Let me talk to my mother," and all of Lewis's calmness fled.

"Now listen, boy," he snapped into the receiver, "I told you your mother isn't here. Now I'm sorry but I have to hang up, I'm expecting......"

But he was cut off by the boy's high, piercing laugh, short and deadly sounding, before he could finish, and then a click and the inevitable buzz of the broken line. He slammed the receiver onto its cradle and shook his head violently.

"What was that all about?" Judy asked. She was standing behind him, beside the table, and when he turned he was startled by the expression on her face, realizing that he must have looked and sounded like a fool. His face flushed and he twisted his mouth into a crooked grin to hide his embarrassment. He and Judy had been married for only six months and they were still going through the sometimes wonderful, sometimes painful process of getting to know each other.

"Just a wrong number," he said.

"Some wrong number."

"Some silly kid, says he's trying to call his mother. He called a few days ago too. I think he's playing a game, dialing numbers at random, trying to shake people up."

"A little boy?" Judy said. She looked doubtful. "Trying to shake people up?" She smiled at him but there was something in her eyes that made his mouth pucker with annoyance. The phone rang before he could say anything. He hesitated, his hand just above the receiver, for a moment before picking it up. It was Stein, the man from his office. When he was finished with the conversation, Judy had forgotten about the boy's call, and they went out for a walk. But Lewis hadn't forgotten, and it preyed on his mind all that evening. He woke the next morning thinking of that terrible laugh.

They lived in a quiet, residential area at the base of Golden Gate Park, just a few blocks from the ocean, and they loved to walk along the beach in the evenings. It was springlike warm, unusually so for the city in April, the rains had all but gone and the days were getting longer. Lewis and Judy would usually go out for a walk after dinner and not be back until after dark, when the streets would become deserted of casual strollers. It was supposed to be unsafe to be on the streets after dark, but after New York, San Francisco seemed tame to them both and often Lewis wished they could walk all night, hating to go back to their house and the waiting for the phone to ring.

In the several weeks after the boy's first two calls he had become a persistent intruder in Lewis's evenings. His reaction to the individual calls oscillated between genuine concern, curiosity, annoyance and, occasionally, anger, but, in general, his uneasiness about the mysterious caller had deepened. Even Judy, who had been skeptical at first, then kidding, after answering the phone a few times before Lewis could get to it, became frightened. Concern for her prompted him to get in touch with the telephone company, but when the man he spoke to there heard that nothing obscene or threatening was being said by the caller he lost interest. Certain that he would be laughed at, Lewis dismissed the idea of talking to the police.

With the exception of the second time, when the boy had called just past dinner time, he invariably called sometime after dark, from as early as 7:30 to as late as midnight. Always, he began by asking to speak to his mother; always, he ended the conversation by laughing and cutting off the line. In between, what he actually said changed subtly from call to call, the message expanding, like a puzzle in which pieces are gradually, painfully filled in.

Lewis's feelings about the boy remained ambivalent even as he grew more apprehensive. Sometimes he would be convinced his caller really was no more than a small boy desperately trying to get through to his mother, thoroughly uncomprehending his difficulty; at other times, Lewis was sure he and Judy were being made the butt of some cruel, perverse prank, perhaps with danger lurking somewhere at the end, and he became frightened. It was an uncomfortable feeling for a grown man, a responsible man, a veteran, a man who had endured the bloodied noses and split lips of streetcorner brawls that seemed inevitably to accompany growing up in New York—to be frightened of a telephone call, of the voice of a small boy. But Lewis sensed poison in that feeble, fuzzy voice, tasted venom in his own mouth when he responded to it, and his heart skipped a beat and sweat stood out on his forehead when he heard the ringing each night.

The calls had become a nightly occurrence. Into them, fairly early, had slipped the character of the boy's father.

"Daddy's coming," the voice whispered. "I must tell my mother."

"Your mother isn't here, Bobby," Lewis said wearily, but he immediately became interested. "Your father is coming? Has he been away? Will he be home soon?"

But the boy would be drawn no further and the laugh came soon, that damned laugh, and the call was over.

"Daddy's coming, he'll be mad if my mother isn't here," the voice said a few calls later.

"Where does your daddy live?" Lewis asked. The boy wouldn't say.

Another time: "Call my mother to the phone, please, my daddy's coming home and I'm frightened."

Lewis, alarmed, spent a wearying five minutes trying to wheedle from the boy where he lived, only to evoke a sobbing, choking sound, screams that he was lying, that the boy's mother *must* be there, ending with the horrible laugh. Lewis, feeling drained and defeated, threw himself face down on the couch and had to struggle to keep sobs from breaking out from his own throat. Judy came and sat beside him, stroking his hair. She didn't ask him what had been said, she had heard half the conversation and she could see the conclusion.

"Let's get our number changed, get an unlisted number," she said. "I'm frightened."

"No," Lewis said. He had already thought about that. But along with the dread growing within him that was personal, directed toward himself and Judy, a fear focusing on the boy was developing. Although he hadn't completely abandoned the idea that the caller was a grown-up or teen-ager, a practical joker or a twisted tormenter, more and more he was becoming convinced that the boy was real, that his calls were pleas for help.

The final call came on a Sunday. It was late, past midnight when the phone rang and Lewis was already in bed, having thought the boy would perhaps spare him one night. He rose on the first ring, like a lifeguard springing from his perch at the first sign of a floundering swimmer, and, perhaps because the calls always made him feel so vulnerable, he took the time to slip into his pants.

He got to the phone on the fifth ring. "Hello?"

He was greeted by a wailing he hadn't encountered before. It was the boy's voice, Bobby's, he knew it well enough now to recognize it no matter how distorted, but it was cracked with fear, swollen with bellowing. "Mommy, Mommy," the voice cried, "save me, Daddy's coming, he's coming up the stairs, he's at the door...." The voice trailed off in a spasm of sobs.

Lewis was alarmed but strangely calm. For once, despite the incoherence of the words which babbled on into his ear, the message of the call was clear—it *was* a call for help, a frightened boy cringing from a threat made of bone and flesh, falling back on the one place where he knew there was a listener. It didn't matter whether his mother was there or not, Lewis was there, and it suddenly dawned on him that, with the possible exception of the first wrong number, the boy never had been calling for his mother, he was calling for Lewis, the nice faceless man who always answered when darkness had come and fear was around him.

"Bobby, Bobby, calm down," Lewis soothed. "It'll be all right, I'm here, I'm listening. Stop crying and tell me what's the matter. What's happened, has your father come home? Is that it?"

But the boy would not be consoled. He kept on sobbing, hiccupping out snatches of words: "Daddy's here.....he's at the door....he's banging.....he's going to kill me......"

"No, no, Bobby," Lewis said softly, firmly, over and over again. Judy had come up behind him, wrapping a robe around her and shivering in the chilly kitchen. "What is it, Lew?" she asked but he didn't hear her, all his attention, all his energy focusing on the telephone, the lifeless receiver through which a life was reaching toward him.

Suddenly Lewis heard a banging, crashing sound in the

background, and the boy's wail pitched higher. He froze, his lips quivering, and now, if he hadn't before, he believed the voice, shared the dread. "What's that noise, Bobby?" he shouted. "What is it? Is it your father?"

"Mommy, Mommy," the voice wailed, "he'll kill me, he'll kill me."

"Bobby, listen to me," Lewis commanded. "What's your name, where do you live? Tell me and I'll call help, I'll come and help you. Do you hear me? Do you understand? Where do you live, what's the address? Bobby, Bobby?"

His voice was drowned out by a heavy, crashing sound, like wood splintering, and the boy's scream. Then there was silence.

"Bobby!" Lewis shouted. "Are you there? Hello, hello, is anybody there? Do you hear me? Answer, for God's sake."

On the other end of the line, someone hung up the phone. The click rang in Lewis's ear like the shot of a pistol, like a hysterical laugh, like a cry of mortal dread. Then came the deadly, endless buzz.

"Oh, my God," Lewis said. He stood dazed, staring at the yellow receiver in his hand as if it were some strange, alien thing he had just discovered, or a powerful talisman which had finally failed him. Judy put her arms around him, draping herself around his bare back, but was silent, trembling. In a moment, he seemed to awaken, pulled himself up straight. Perhaps it wasn't too late, something could be done. If only he knew where the boy lived, knew his last name. Why hadn't he, in all these weeks, done more than just listen, why hadn't he pumped the information he needed so desperately now out of the boy? Why hadn't he cared enough to try to answer?

It didn't matter now, he knew; it was too late for bullying himself. He had to do something, *now*. What was that name? The boy, several times, had said he'd gotten the number from a woman. Mrs. Anderson? No, Andrews. That was it. Mrs. Andrews. He reached for the phone book, in a drawer beneath the phone but stopped before he had it out. There must be hundreds of Andrews. The number? Surely, the first time, the boy must have dialed the number wrong or, if he had it written down, it was written wrong.

He looked at the number on the phone. Seven numerals, any one of the could be the key. Perhaps if he tried calling a few, changing a numeral each time? No, there were too many possibilities, thousands of alternatives.

He reached for the dial, meaning to call the operator and ask for the police, but shame stopped him. In the end, he went forlornly into the street, barefooted and shirtless, shivering in the cold, to stand in front of the house, staring up and down the dark, silent street as if there was something to see, as if something would be revealed in the light from the streetlamp, the neon at the gas station on the corner. He wanted to cry out but was silent. He wanted to walk barechested to the ocean and stare out across the dark water until dawn came up, but he was afraid. After a few minutes Judy came out, put her face against his chest and led him into the house.

TRUCKEE YOUR BLUES AWAY

They stopped for gas in Elko and Bruce suggested coffee. "It's a long way to Reno and I need it."

"How about right here?" Lena asked. There was a cafe next to the gas station, with two semi-trailers and rigs parked outside.

"Oh, let's check out one of the places."

Lena shook her head. "We'll be in Reno tonight."

"We need coffee anyway."

"We'll never get to the coast," Lena said. She shrugged, smiling, and Bruce started the car.

"What's your hurry, anyway? We're on holiday."

They followed the neon lights to a gaudy casino-hotel called The Silver Slipper where a giant grubstaker beckoned to them with a glittering pan of gold in one hand, a pistol in the other and a luminescent leer on his grotesque face. You had to walk through his legs to get to the door. Inside, an ancient woman, the used up flesh hanging like baggy drapes from her bones, sat wearily hunched on a camp stool at a belching slot machine, feeding nickel after nickel into the blind bandit from an overflowing tray at its gaping mouth, a faded expression of boredom and idiocy blending in her shallow, yellowish eyes. Fascinated, Bruce took up a position behind another machine, wasting a handful of nickels, to stare at the woman while Lena went to the can.

"Who's your girlfriend?" she asked when they were seated in a booth out of the din and glare of the main room. She reached for a menu but was distracted by a Keno card and a set of rules stacked in a pile next to the sugar bowl and salt and pepper setting.

"She's weird, okay," Bruce said. "Did you see her? Christ, I watched her for five minutes and her expression never changed. She didn't look at the machine, the nickels, nothing."

"This is a weird place," Lena said, her shoulders rising slightly in a shrug. "A weird state, a weird country. I can't make anything out of this."

They studied the Keno rules until the waitress came and they ordered coffee. Lena asked for a piece of blueberry pie.

"Pie for you?" The waitress was a small, compactly built girl, probably younger than Lena but older looking, with dark hair swirled into an elaborate concoction surrounding her head and dark, narrow eyes thick with mascara beneath exaggerated brows. She gave off a faint fragrance of dead flowers.

"No thanks, I'm driving," Bruce said, smiling.

The girl made a face and wheeled around with a subtle grace. He watched her hips recede behind the long plastic counter, then linked his eyes to Lena's. "So this is Nevada," he said, rolling his eyes.

"Italian?" Lena asked.

"I don't get you."

"The waitress, your new girlfriend. Is she Italian?"

"Could be, dark enough, and looked hot-blooded. And she had purple eyelids. Is that a giveaway?"

She made an exasperated sound and smiled. "How long've we been married?"

"I'm not sure. Seven, eight years...wait, eight. Why?"

"Some memory. Don't you remember our Italian waitress joke?"

"Oh, yeah, you were gonna get me an Italian waitress for my birthday or something like that. I'm surprised *you* remembered."

"That's not the kind of thing women forget," Lena said, her smile receding slightly. Her fine-boned face was pale, the slight lines around her eyes etched deeper by tiredness. "For a time,

I was really thinking seriously about doing it, getting you one. Then I figured if you really wanted one badly enough you'd take care of it yourself.'' She paused, started to say something else, then checked herself. The waitress came back, saving her from having to go on.

Bruce smiled at the waitress, murmured a ''thank you'' but avoided her eyes. The lids really were purple, he noticed as he lowered his head over his cup. When she was gone, he raised his eyes to find Lena watching him. ''I haven't thought about that for a long time,'' he said simply. Then, after a moment: ''Why is that something you wouldn't forget? Because I wanted one or because you wanted me to have it?''

They looked at each other for a long moment, their eyes steady. Then Lena shrugged and picked up her fork.

On their way out, they paused in the casino to watch the merciless woman in her bored assault on the slot machine. Nothing of the scene had changed, neither the pile of nickels in the tray, the hunch of her shoulders, the piston-like movement of her arm as she grasped the rubber-tipped handle and brought it down, the jangling flash of the machine itself as its three blind eyes spun through their changes, nor the dazed, opaque expression of her eyes.

''Do you suppose she's always been sitting there, forever, or does she have a past?'' Lena asked as they walked to the car. The sun had gone down and dusk was sinking around them.

''Like that Greek who had to push the rock up the mountain,'' Bruce said. That wasn't exactly what he meant, he realized, but he made no effort to correct himself.

They drove for several miles in silence, watching the receding horizon grow dark over the stark dry mountains. Purple clouds caught the final rays of shattered sunlight and spun them through the windshield, blinding him. He lit a cigarette and drove with one hand, his free elbow propped up on the open window, his hand cupped over his eyes, smoke curling gently down on his pensive face.

''What are you thinking about?'' Lena asked. She was sitting close to him, her knees bent and her feet beneath her on the seat.

She'd loosened her hair and was massaging her throat with the bandana she'd taken from around her head.

"Nothing," Bruce said, turning to her, smiling. "I was just thinking...no, nothing." He turned back to the road.

"What?"

"Oh, just...I understand prostitution's legal in Nevada. This would be a good time for you to get me that birthday present."

"It's not your birthday," Lena said coolly. She frowned slightly, the color rising almost unnoticeably to her high cheeks, and placed a slim hand on his head, tousling his hair. "So I guess you lose again."

"Guess so," Bruce said. They grinned at each other and he gripped her hand, squeezing it. She turned on the radio.

It was almost 2 a.m. when the lights of Sparks and Reno came flashing down the highway toward them, drawing them forward like a chain attached to the front bumper of the car pulling them through a tunnel of darkness to the far lighted exit. They passed cheap looking motels with *vacancy* signs glowing dimly. The searchlight atop Harrah's pulled them deeper into the city, their eyes widening.

"What a fucking town," Bruce said.

They crossed a bridge over the Truckee River and they could see the mist rising off the water in the glare of headlamps. "Keep on truckee, Momma," Lena said, laughing.

"Truckee your blues away," he answered.

It was a Tuesday and Bruce wanted to take a chance on going downtown without a reservation. Lena sighed but didn't protest. The traffic on Virginia Avenue was thick so he went two blocks further before turning left. They saw the lights of the Arlington Plaza and pulled onto the drive ramp. He stopped the car in front of the lobby and a bellman came trotting out through the swinging doors, a fabricated smile building on his grey face.

"Any vacancies?" Bruce asked.

The bellman cocked his head. The tag on his left breast pocket said "Pinky." He was short and wiry, with brown hands and a deep cleft in his chin. "You'll have to ask at the desk, sir," he said. "But I think there're a few nice rooms left." He winked.

Bruce went inside the lobby and talked to a blonde woman with an oddly twisted mouth. She checked them in. Pinky brought in the overnight bag and Lena checked the lock on the trunk, then followed him. A painfully thin boy with pimples on his forehead took the car keys.

Their room was on the eleventh floor, facing the heart of the city and its still pulsating lights, with a king-sized bed and an attractive black leatherette love seat. "Very nice," Bruce said. He gave the bellman a dollar.

He sat on the loveseat while Lena showered, the drapes open, staring out at the city, smoking a cigarette slowly and letting the tiredness seep gently out of his body. This was their fourth day on the road. When the cigarette had burned down to his fingers he lit another.

Lena came padding up behind him, wrapped in a towel. "It's beautiful," she said.

"Want to go out and have a drink?"

"Oh, wow, are you crazy? It's bed for me. You go if you want to, but don't forget we're supposed to be in San Francisco at dinner time tomorrow, and it's still a few hours drive. Aren't you tired?"

"Yeah, I'm bushed." He shrugged, crushed out the cigarette and took off his shirt. He watched her through narrow eyes as she put on her nightgown, his gaze following the sweep of her arms as they raised high above her head, her breasts flattened by the lifting motion. The nightgown tumbled down her body, past her tight slim belly and over the soft flow of her hips.

Lena smiled at him. "What are you looking at?"

"Just looking."

"Aren't you going to take a shower?"

"Yeah, I guess so." He stripped and stood naked for a moment at the window, wondering if anyone could see him. He didn't think so. He heard the rustle of the sheets as Lena crawled into bed.

"This is terrific," she said.

He went into the bathroom and showered quickly. When he

came out he paused beside the bed and looked down at her face. Her eyes were closed and he could hear the steady, easy rhythm of her breathing. A strand of her dark hair covered one eye like a bruise. He crawled in beside her, rolled across the big bed until he was pressed up against her back and touched her neck gently.

"I'm asleep," Lena said.

Bruce laughed and rolled over, sighing loudly. After a moment, he said, "You in any terrific hurry to get to the city?"

There was a long silence. Bruce began to count to himself, slowly. "You know we're supposed to be at the Knudsons' tomorrow night," she said finally.

"We're on holiday. What's *supposed to* mean?"

"Oh, I don't care. Do what you like. I'm just along for the ride."

He could hear her screwing her face into the pillow, as if trying to flee from him into feathers. He wanted to touch her again but he didn't. He lay on his back, his head propped up slightly on the pillow, staring out the window across the room at the beacon which pulsed from the top of Harrah's. "I thought I might take a chance on one of those Italian waitresses tomorrow," he said.

"You bastard."

"Hey, I'm only kidding."

"Close the drapes, please. If we're going to stay, we might as well get some sleep in the morning. The light will wake us up."

"Okay," he said. He got out of bed and padded silently across the room, then back to bed in darkness.

Something in the air—neither heat nor light—seemed to wake him, something as ephemeral as the city itself, breathing in his ear. He went to the window and peered through the drapes, looking down on empty streets, across a midtown as drab and dreary-looking as any city's by day, the sun bright in his narrow eyes as it climbed over the dry brown mountains to the east. He felt alone, like someone who wakes up in a cramped Greyhound seat to find the bus empty, rows of suitcases staring down forlornly at him from their racks. On his way to the bathroom, he glanced at his watch on the bedtable; it was 10:15. The loneliest time of all in this town, he thought, after the last losers have gone home to bed to nurse their wounds and the first arrivals haven't stirred yet from theirs with fresh hopes. Like three in the morning in any other town.

He showered, brushed his teeth, shaved and brushed his hair carefully, with a minimum amount of noise. He dressed in slacks, fresh shirt and a sports jacket, omitting the tie, and slipped into black loafers, then tiptoed into the bedroom to scoop his keys, loose change and wallet off the dresser.

"Where are you going?" Lena asked sleepily. She was curled in the bed facing him, her face puffed with sleep, hair tangled. Her eyes were only half-open and her words were blurred.

He grinned at her as he strapped the watch on. "I'm going downtown to shake up a little action. Go back to sleep. I'll be back in a few hours."

She sighed, moved uncertainly under the covers, then lifted herself onto a crooked elbow. "Wait for me, I'll go along." Her eyes opened wider, blinking.

"The hell you will. Go back to sleep. I told you, I'm going to try my luck with one of those waitresses." The grin was fixed on his pale face and his voice was soft. "I've always been a law-abiding sort but here it's legal. Why should you care anyway? It'll save you having to buy me a present this year." He leaned over the bed and kissed the top of her head. "Go back to sleep. I'll be back in a few hours."

He didn't wait for a reply, turning on his heels and heading for the door. He had the room key in his jacket pocket. He took the elevator down, nodded to the two girls at the main desk and went out through the lobby door, turning left and taking a deep breath of the hot, dry air.

At the corner of West and Second he glanced up at the street signs to get his bearings, then headed right on Second, letting the towering Harrah's building be his guide. For the first block, Second was like a fringe-of-downtown street anywhere, with a grocery, a drug store, a radio and TV repair shop. On the next block, the neon began, first with a pawn shop, then a bar marquee advertising topless dancers and an arrow pointing down an alley. On the next street there were two more topless bars. He stopped in front of the first one and peered in the doorway. The room was dark, reeking of sweat and alcohol. He walked on and turned left on Virginia, crossing both streets diagonally and heading for Harrah's.

The slot machine area of the casino was more crowded than he'd thought it would be. He cashed in a dollar for a roll of nickels and wandered aimlessly through the rows of jangling machines and weary looking middle-aged women, shoving his coins randomly into a slot here and there, pulling at handles absently. His palm grew moist from the clammy metal he cradled as he walked. On one machine he hit a small pay-out and found himself grinning idiotically in a wall mirror as nickel after nickel came spitting out into the tray, ringing hollowly. He scooped them up with his free hand and counted fourteen, then fed them methodically back into the machine.

Back on the street outside, he had to blink his eyes in the sharp light. Foot traffic was thickening already and taxis clogged the street. He dodged across to the Silver Spur and went to the bar. He had a bloody Mary, lit a cigarette and sat on a stool with his back to the bar, letting his eyes wander across the smoky room. There were large paintings of nude women hanging on the walls, young, fresh-faced, high-breasted realistically painted women with ornate hats and feather boas draped around their necks. Their nipples were unnaturally large, unhealthily pink. A live woman in tight pink shorts and a halter passed by him, jostling his elbow.

"Sorry," she said, smiling. Her blonde face was as sharp and unreal as those of the girls in the paintings.

"That's all right," Bruce said, swiveling on his stool.

He ordered another bloody Mary and sipped at it as he wandered across the room and downstairs, standing for several minutes over a blackjack table watching a chain-smoking Chinese man and a sharply dressed middle-aged man with a flat midwestern accent and a slick pompadour play against a wry-mouthed, red-haired dealer in an ill-fitting uniform dress. The dealer cocked her head at him as she raked in chips and smiled wryly. "Sit down, take a load off."

"Maybe later," Bruce said.

He went out and wandered down Virginia, going from one club to another without staying long at any. Across the street, at the Primadonna, he bought ten dollars worth of chips, a bourbon on the rocks like the man beside him at the bar, a lean, sandy-faced man with a tight collar and a broad-brimmed hat, was having, and prowled the floor until he found a blackjack table empty. The dealer was a short blonde girl with clear blue eyes and good breasts. She was shuffling, a bored expression on her face. She smiled quickly when Bruce sat down, shoving a coaster across the table to him, then an ashtray when he lit a cigarette. She said nothing. Bruce raised the corners of his lips in greeting.

He bet two chips, drew an eighteen and held. She went over. He left the four chips in the circle, then promptly lost them when he pulled a sixteen and got a queen on his first hit.

He slid two more chips into the circle. The girl shuffled the cards and he cut. The white tag on her left breast said "Wendy." He won on a twenty, stayed with the four chips and won again on an eighteen. The girl frowned slightly as she stacked the chips on his pile.

"Tough racket, eh?"

She smiled. "Not too tough."

She shuffled and he tapped the deck. The girl's eyes were large, with no trace of make-up. One eyebrow was slightly crooked, with a slight bump in the clear skin above it, perhaps the result of an old hurt. He drew a king and a jack and grinned as he slid the cards under his pile of chips. The girl went over with a twenty-four.

"Been here long?" he asked.

"The club or Reno?"

"Reno."

"A few months."

"Like it?"

The girl shrugged. "It's better than Moline."

Bruce laughed. She flicked cards at him and he peeked under their edges. "Hit." She dealt him a four and he nodded. She dealt herself another card, frowned and counted out two stacks of chips. He counted his winnings and slid all but five of his chips next to his empty glass. "Buy you a drink?"

"Sure." She turned her head. "Frank?"

The pitboss came up beside her, a tall, swarthy man with thick lips. The upper lip, which he curled at Bruce, looked like it had been split some time ago and was almost completely healed. "Bourbon and ice," Bruce said and looked at the girl. "Same," she said quietly.

He lost the five chips on the next deal when he stayed with eighteen and she hit twenty-one. He bet two more and lost again. The drinks came and he finished his quickly when a heavy woman in a green sweater, green slacks and green eyeshade sat down on the end stool. He scooped his remaining chips into a cupped hand and nodded at the girl. "Thanks, Wendy."

"Anytime." Her smile faded before he turned away.

He cashed in his chips, $27 worth, and put the bills in his wallet. Outside, the hot air brought moisture to his forehead. The street was crowded. He walked up Virginia behind two girls in tight blue jeans, watching the easy sway of their hips, and turned right on Second. He stopped at a jewelry store, scanned the window and went inside. A grey-haired woman with a pinched face smiled at him from the other side of the glass counter. "May I help you, sir?" Her dress looked like something his mother had once worn.

"I'd like to see a necklace in the window. It's jade. I'll show you." He led the woman to the entranceway so he could point it out. It was a nicely carved stone, Indian work, on a thin gold chain. He examined it under a strong light in the shop and paid $35 for it.

"I should have stayed at the table a little longer," he said.

"I beg your pardon?"

"Nothing, just a joke. Could you gift wrap it please?"

"Surely, sir. Do you wish to enclose a card?"

He hesitated. "Yeah, sure, if you have something blank."

She brought him a small folded card with a flower printed on the front. He found a ball-point next to the cash register and scribbled "Happy birthday, baby" inside the card. He put the card in a small pink envelope and folded the flap inside. The grey-haired woman fastened the envelope under the ribbon she tied expertly around the small package. A red bow went on last.

"Thank you," Bruce said. He went out and continued down Second, pausing to cross the street and peer again into the topless bar. A slim girl with long white hair danced lazily on the poorly lit stage. She wore black bikini panties and black slippers. Her breasts were slim, pear-shaped, firm. Her hair dangled over her shoulders, reaching to the tips of her breasts. The girl's eyes were closed and her shoulders swayed slowly. Bruce stood in the doorway watching her until the song ended and the jukebox began to whirr. The girl stopped, raised her chin and shook her head lazily. She looked at him with disinterest and he moved on.

The bellman was on duty in the lobby. They nodded to each other and Bruce rang for the elevator. "Sure hot out," he said.

"It's always like that," Pinky said. "This time of year, it's always like that." The cleft in the man's chin seemed deeper than it had been the night before, and his eyes had a pink sheen around the lashes, as if a night's rest had sharpened his features, put him more finely into focus.

The elevator door opened and Bruce nodded and went in. He whistled softly as the leather-padded cage rose. The whistle grew louder as he walked down the hall to their room, a slightly off-key version of a song they'd heard on the car radio the night before. He paused at the door to listen for a moment, then turned the key and went in.

"Hey, hon, wake up. I'm back." He went through the narrow corridor which passed the bathroom and opened onto the bedroom. The room was empty.

"Lena?" He backtracked into the bathroom, calling her name again. The shower stall was damp but fresh towels hung neatly on the racks beside it.

He went back to the bedroom, looking at his watch. It was just past two. The bed had been made and the ashtrays cleaned. All traces of their occupancy—stray shoes, Lena's handbag, hair pins—were out of sight. He stood in the middle of the room, looking around him, a small package with a ribbon and a red bow in his hand, a feeling of familiar emptiness beginning to grow in the pit of his stomach. He opened the top drawer of the dresser. Except for a Gideon's Bible and some hotel stationery, it was empty.

He dropped the package into the drawer and closed it quietly.

He went into the bathroom, saw with a glance that the sink was bare of combs, brushes, shaving kit and the like, and turned to the closet. Hangers swayed forlornly from their fixed rod, bare and mocking. The suitcase was gone from the shelf. In the corner, on the floor, was a crumpled paper bag. He carried it into the bedroom and dumped its contents on the bed: the shirt and jeans he'd worn the day before, a pair of dirty underpants and dirty socks, his toothbrush, razor, comb and brush.

He sat on the bed beside the clutter and sighed heavily.

"Damn," he said softly.

He sat there for several minutes gazing across the room and through the window at the city. The neon was dead but through the clear still air he could read lettering on signs blocks away. Directly in his vision was a tall, gleaming black building with no signs, more like an office building than a club or a hotel. He wondered idly what it was, what was going on behind its windowless walls right at that moment.

He went downstairs, putting on his sunglasses in the elevator. The bellman looked up as he emerged into the lobby.

"I'd like my car," Bruce said.

"Yes, sir," Pinky said. "Have the ticket?"

He slapped at his shirt pocket absently. "I guess I lost it. A green Chrysler, Manitoba plates. I'll recognize the keys."

The bellman turned to a board lined with keys on pegs and studied it for a moment. "Oh, I remember now. The lady took it, about an hour ago."

"The lady?"

"Your wife," Pinky said hesitantly. His eyes were a startling dark brown. They seemed to grow darker with doubt.

"Oh, that's right. She said..." Bruce let the sentence trail off. He shrugged his shoulders and grinned faintly. "That's all right. I don't need it."

He nodded to the bellman and started to turn away.

"Just a second sir, she left this envelope for you."

Bruce was staring at the cleft in Pinky's chin as he reached for the envelope. If you slipped, he thought, you could fall into that

thing and never be found. "Thanks." He went outside and stood
in front of the hotel while he slit the envelope open with a finger-
nail. There was a note inside, written in Lena's careful script on
a sheet of blue hotel stationery.

"Decided to go on and have dinner with the Knudsons as
planned. Knew you wouldn't mind. Have a happy birthday and
come on when you feel like it. Keep on Truckee." There was no
signature.

He closed his eyes and laughed softly, then the laugh turned
into a curse—not for her nor for himself, but an undirected oath
which sounded familiar to him but peculiar at the same time,
like an answer to a question no one had asked. He folded the note,
put it back in the envelope and tucked that into his inside breast
pocket. Then he straightened his chin and turned left, heading
for Second.

He didn't pause at the entrance but went right in and found
a stool at the bar. In the mirror behind the bottles he could see
the empty stage. A thick woman with bleached blonde hair was
wiping her hands on a towel down the bar. When she came up,
he ordered a bourbon on the rocks. A few men were sitting at
a table near the stage with a girl in underwear, the long-haired
blonde he had seen dancing before. Otherwise, the place was
empty. A scratchy country and western song played on the jukebox.
He drank the bourbon in one gulp and ordered another and a
glass of water. The whiskey tasted awful. After awhile, the girl
in the underwear came and sat on the stool beside him. She was
wearing the same black panties and a lacy black bra to match.
She smelled faintly of dead flowers. Her eyes were small and almost
hidden behind long lashes.

"Buy a working girl a drink?" she asked. She was smiling.

"Sure," Bruce said. Despite the color of her hair, she was Italian,
he supposed.

MISTER MAESTRO

Mister Maestro was an average-sized man with hourglass hips and hairy wrists, a vain man without reason, a man with much to say who talked little.

His hips and wrists were of considerable concern to him for much of his life, the first because he feared they made him look soft, which they did, to a certain extent; the second because he feared they made him look animalistic, which they certainly did not. There was little he could do about his hips, which were more to do with bone than tissue, but he developed a nervous habit, as he approached middle age, of tugging down the cuffs of his Paris-made silk and linen shirts in hopes of masking the thick curly tufts of black hair which grew like snakeweed toward his palms. But, rather than help, this merely called attention to what he sought to hide.

The truth was, as it so often is with people overly concerned about their appeaarance, that Mister Maestro was a perfectly ordinary looking individual whom people rarely took notice of. Few people, if any, ever snickered about those blights on his image. The fact that he was an arsonist, a womanizer and—bluntly—a cold prick was far more noticeable.

Also of note was the curious coincidence that all the people he surrounded himself with were fat. His wife, Merrillee, was fat, uncontrollably, unrepentantly fat; as was his son, Tush, and his daughter, Thorne, who was self-consciously, miserably fat and had begun the last of a seemingly endless—though it obviously wasn't—series of diets only days before she died. His mother-in-law, Zee, who lived with them so long there were times when Mister Maestro could barely remember whether it was mother or daughter he had married, was *stout*, that was the word for it, not fat, because, though she was huge, with breasts like pillows and hips like snowdrifts, she was solid, and her condition, so long a part of her she could not remember a time when she was ever slim, caused her not the slightest concern. Even Mister Maestro's long-time business partner in film production, aluminum siding and other matters, Sydney Lumut—no relation to the movie director—was fat; in fact, he was a grotesque man, no taller than five-foot-three and almost as wide, with a fringed bald pate and a perpetual frown that made him look like a constipated Friar Tuck. Surrounded by these mountains of excess, Mister Maestro himself was like a lean and sinewy, if average-sized and wide-hipped, solitary peak.

He was a photographer by trade, which is to say that is the trade the army taught him. His first name was Lemuel, which he understood came from the Bible, and he was called Lem in the army, an improvement over the nickname he had acquired as a child, which was Lemon. His last name was Meister, which easily made the transition to Maestro when he opened his first studio after the war. It sounded more artistic, and also more Italian, which he found seemed to make a difference to women.

This was all in Cleveland, which he left rather suddenly following a certain fire. In later years, he spoke rarely about that phase of his life, and not at all about his youth, so Merrillee could only guess at the possible dark and tumultuous forces which had helped shape him. Since she had always called him Mister, she wasn't even sure about his proper given name. And she herself, of course, had begun life as Myrna, with few of the aspirations and none of the comforts he was to lead her to.

Myrna was eighteen, slender and vaguely pretty when she met

him, during the Coney Island phase of his career. She, like most of the girls on her block, worked at the hat factory; he was the dark, curly-haired fellow who had opened up the portrait studio on the next corner over, where Stein's haberdashery had been. She and her friends passed the studio on their way to the factory in the morning and on their way home in the evening, and at both times of day they could see him through the window, acting busy behind his counter but watching them. Sometimes he smiled and the girls put their hands to their faces and giggled. The sign in the window said: *Mister Maestro, individual and group portraits, the camera brandished like a painter's brush—your face in a work of art.*

On a Friday evening in spring, she worked late and was rushing home alone to light the candles for her mother, who wouldn't touch a match past noon. There was a light on in the studio and she paused at the window, pretending to be studying the portraits hanging against a black background but actually peering over them for a glimpse of him. So intent was she in her search that she didn't hear the tinkle of the bell as he opened the door beside her.

"Come in and I'll take your picture."

"Oh, my God." She jumped, her hands flying to her breasts as if to ward off an attack. "You startled me."

He was smiling and one curl had dipped forward over his right eye. He was leaning against the doorjamb so that his lower body was in shadow, and his hands were behind his back. Since Myrna was petite, he appeared tall, and very lean and hard, like something it would be exciting to rub against and hug. She wondered if it was true, as some of the girls said with assurance, that he was an Italian.

"Don't be frightened," he said. "I'm sorry, I didn't mean to frighten you. Come on, come in and I'll take your picture."

"Oh, I can't afford...." She looked down, embarrassed.

"No, for free. Listen, you'd be doing me a favor. A portrait of a pretty girl like you in the window, it'll bring in plenty of business for me."

Myrna blushed, tittered. She wanted to protest, mostly so that he would insist, but she was too embarrassed even for that. "I've got to get home, my mother will be wondering where I am."

"This won't take long."

"No, I'm late already. I've got to light the candles."

"Come back later. I'll be here till late."

"It's *Friday*, I can't"

"Come tomorrow, then. In the afternoon, if you like, or in the evening." He could see her considering. "Tell your mother you're going to the pictures with a girl friend. The *pictures*, get it? I'll be here all day."

He smiled as she ran off and rolled his sleeves again, went inside only to turn off the light.

She came the next afternoon, shy and blushing, slender and a virgin. Neither condition lasted long. Later, when she grew fat, her interest in it and his interest in her waned. There were no more men in Myrna's life but there were many women in his, though they seemed to mean little. He pursued them out of weary habit, rubbed against them, pushed into them out of duty or reflex, like a man eating to satisfy his jaws, not his belly. And there was never anything, any one, to match the intensity of that afternoon, the way the head and shoulders portrait stretched into the full-length nude study, the way the artistic detachment melted into a throbbing they thought would split their heads. He would try, sometimes, years later, to remember the whiteness of her skin—not whiteness like the underside of a fish or the soft centre of a loaf of fresh bread, but whiteness like snow or feathers from a torn pillow—and the darkness of her hair, the lustre of her eyes as he moved the camera closer, closer, the smell of her like one certain spot in the bakery his father had worked in in Dayton—not *all* of the bakery, just one special spot—and the softness of her, the newness. But it was hard to remember *that* when Merrillee jiggled at him over the breakfast table and the children were crying, and his mind was on other things.

Kittycorner from the photo studio was Larry's candy store, where bookies, pimps, guys between jobs and the neighborhood kids hung out. Mister Maestro used to go there to have a grilled cheese with tomato and an egg cream for lunch, and there he met Syd, who had always been short and was already starting to blossom.

"I saw," Syd said. He sat down at the counter beside Mister Maestro and held up a finger to Larry signifying coffee.

"Yeah?" Mister Maestro said without interest. He was reading the racing story in the folded *Mirror* by his elbow.

"Yeah. I mean, I *saw*. What you did."

Mister Maestro looked up, chewing.

Syd tapped him on the thigh. "Putting that big thing right in the middle of that little girl, the poor girl." He rolled his eyes in a lewd expression Mister Maestro would come to know well in the years to come. "I bet it hurt plenty. *Ooh, ooh, that hurts.* Say, if I were her father, I'd kill you."

Mister Maestro stared at him, his mouth open, a thin trail of tomato sliding toward his chin. He was visualizing the studio, the back room, the bare white walls, the door leading to the alley, the small window in it, the tattered green window shade.

"But she don't have no father, lucky for you," Syd said. He was slurping his coffee, inspecting with wide eyes the Danish pastries in the round plastic tray on the counter.

"No?"

"Naw. Just a rich mother." He gestured toward the Danish tray, catching Larry's eye, then helped himself to a piece oozing with cherries.

Mister Maestro examined the plump man beside him who was now noisily chewing. It was obvious he knew—he *had* seen, somehow, and God only knows what else he had seen through the holes in the shade. He himself had never used the sofa in the studio before, but other people had, while he clicked away. Part of the service was the guarantee of confidentiality. And now?

"Rich?" he asked distractedly.

"Well, maybe not *rich*. But with plenty of money." Syd's tongue darted out like an anteater's to nab a falling cherry. "Enough."

Mister Maestro considered the situation. He could easily kill the little fat punk—that was another trade the army had taught him, although he hadn't had a chance to practise it except under the most harrowing of conditions—and he had no scruples about doing so. But something the gross balding man had just said interested him.

"What did you say?"

"You heard me. Enough. I said enough."

"And what do you want?" Mister Maestro asked.

"Me? I don't want nothin'." Syd made a face that created a reasonable impression of a turnip left too long in the grocer's bin.

"Come on, you fat fart. Don't fuck me around. What you're telling me I could kill you for."

"Easy, my friend, take it easy." Syd placed a plump hand on Mister Maestro's seersucker arm. "A consideration, that's all I ask. You have something to sell, maybe, I have some experience as a salesman. You have something you're having trouble finding, me, I know where to find some things. A consideration, that's all. You, my friend, are a man with a future. I can see that."

"That's true," Mister Maestro said. He was, in fact, convinced of that, though unsure of the direction that future would take.

"And as you go through life, through its ups and downs, across the forests and glens, over hills and dales—"

"Jesus," Mister Maestro said.

"—through the good times and the bad, you'll need, sometimes, to have a friend. And that is all I ask. That that friend be me."

Mister Maestro looked at the cherry-smeared mouth hanging only inches from his face. "Why?" he asked, incredulously.

Syd laughed. When he did that, Mister Maestro was to notice over the years to come, the adam's apple normally buried in the fat folds of his neck became visible. "You let me worry about that, my friend. *You* worry about your future."

Part of it, that future, was the children, of course. Tush was the first born, but Thorne was the apple of Mister Maestro's eye, becoming, at least for a while, the one genuine receptacle in his world for his affection. He played with her, told her stories, bought her toys she quickly discarded, frilly dresses that rarely fit. To repay him for this outpouring, the little girl, who Mister Maestro, in a fit of inspiration, had named after the man who wrote those books about the ghosts, performed the one feat predetermined to bring it to an end, grew fat. But, while it lasted, Tush glowered, keeping his own counsel. He was a generally cheerful boy, named Sydney, after his father's business associate, the film distributor, who became, in an unofficial capacity, his godfather, but he soon acquired the nickname he wasn't to lose until law school, by persisting in baring his behind, like the time, as Myrna and Zee sat on the front stoop hoping for a breeze from the ocean, baby Thorne sucking her plump thumb in the carriage beside them, he slid down his short pants and underpants and sat down in a puddle beneath the curb older children had created by opening the fire hydrant earlier in the day.

"Sydney, darling, what are you doing?" Zee asked in wonder.

"Cooling off my tush," the boy said, pushing peals of laughter out of the stout grandmother.

"Mama, Mama, this is nothing to laugh at," Myrna said. Though she was still far away from becoming Merrillee, already there was a whine in her voice. "He could catch pneumonia."

But it was Thorne who was the sickly one. She had croup, measles, chicken pox and mumps, and always the worst case in the school, keeping her home in bed for weeks at a time, the bedroom the children shared with Zee dark and moist from the hot water bottles and the pots of water on the radiator. During the summer, the three-room flat on Rockaway Avenue Zee had inherited from her father stank of the punk sticks Myrna burned around the clock to ward off polio, and they seemed to work. Thorne was home from school, her face swollen to twice its size by an abscessed tooth, the day the hat factory burned down, and she and Myrna and Zee stood in the window watching the fire trucks race down the street, watched the flames and smoke and heat press up against the sky, like a hand pushing back the oppressive day.

"Thank God in heaven you don't work there anymore," Zee said.

"Mama, I haven't worked there for years."

"No thanks to Mister."

"Mama, it's not his fault people have no money to waste on portraits these days."

"Waste is the correct word."

"That's not fair, Mama. Mister does good work. He's an artist. People don't appreciate. You should see the magazines at the studio, photo magazines. He does pictures just as good. But times are hard now. They'll get better. Syd says there are big things ahead for Mister."

Zee shivered. A burst of flames turned the sky orange and they watched in silence for a moment.

"But Mister was probably right, I should have gone back to work," Myrna said. "Now, he says, I don't gotta, things are getting better."

"Well, thank God in heaven it wasn't at the hat factory," Zee said.

"They wouldn't have hired me anyway. Business has been bad."

"So what else is new?" Zee asked.

But things did get better, and soon, just like Syd had prophesied. Mister and Syd went into aluminum siding for themselves ("this is the coming thing, believe me," Syd said) and before they knew it, they were in a big house in Manasqua Park, each with a bedroom of their own, and stainless steel cutlery on the table. One day, Myrna, who was now called Merrillee, called the children to dinner and Thorne didn't respond.

"Thorne, Thorne, I'll give you such a smack if you don't get down here," Merrillee shouted at the bottom of the stairs.

"I'll go see," Zee said, and she labored up the stairs, her chest heaving, and found the poor child lying motionless on the bed. Her scream brought them all running, even Mister Maestro, who had been carving the roast and had meat juice on the towel he'd tucked into his belt.

"Maybe if she had a more normal life," Merrillee said after the doctor had come and gone. There was nothing actually wrong, he said. Just a weakness. It would pass, most likely.

"Normal?" Mister Maestro said. "What could be more normal?" He gestured around the spacious livingroom, with its overstuffed chairs and sofas, end tables, knickknack chests and television set. There was an oil painting of the Brooklyn Bridge above the fireplace.

"Maybe if she had a real girl's name," Merrillee complained irrationally.

"Jesus," Mister Maestro snorted, rolling his eyes upward. But

he had opened his *Times* and Merrillee didn't see the expression.
"Like Myrna, maybe?"

"No," Merrillee whined, sulking.

Three weeks later, the girl collapsed at the dining room table
and another doctor was called, one who brought in a specialist,
a doctor who'd once seen FDR. Thorne went into hospital and
they sucked fluid out of her like mosquitoes in July. "I've never
seen this in someone so young," the Roosevelt doctor said.
"Parkinson's disease. Incredible. It usually only attacks older
people. I'd like to do more tests. This is remarkable." He peered
suspiciously at Mister Maestro. "Any history of this in your
family?"

"Parker's disease? No, of course not," he answered quickly,
as if it were so.

With a room of her own, Zee's attitude toward Mister Maestro
changed. Her husband had been a sign painter named Trotsky
(he was a second cousin of the great man) who ran away when
Myrna was still a baby and she had spent the rest of her youth
and most of her middle age caring for her widowed father, a stone-
faced tailor with a sense of humor like a shark's. He operated a
prosperous business but he had a weakness for women and his
mistresses had left him penniless. When he died, all he left to
Zee was the lease to the tiny apartment in Coney Island. Syd's
mistaken assessment of her wealth was based on a general belief
in the neighborhood that the old man, who lived into his eighties,
had amassed a fortune but chose to live like a miser. Even Syd
didn't know about the mistresses her father kept in an apartment
building on Ocean Parkway where the dentist he often visited had
his office.

Mister Maestro's hopes of falling heir to the inheritance kept
alive for many years, though, until past the time when he could
barely remember what it was all about, and he made her old age
a happy one, something Merrillee was always grateful for, despite
everything else. When Tush ran off to Mississippi and Merrillee
was hysterical, Zee was calm and comforted him.

"That boy has a head on his shoulders," she said, putting her
hand on Mister Maestro's shoulder after they read the note he

left. "He'll keep his eyes open and out of trouble."

"You think I give a shit what happens to him?" Mister Maestro snapped. "He can go to hell for all I care if this is all he thinks of his family."

But he did care—to his own surprise—and his complaint was really for Merrillee's benefit, to help her justify the panic she felt. But as her panic grew, with the delivery of each day's newspaper, he found himself feeling less sympathy for it all the time. Tush didn't write for a long time, and whenever there was something on the TV news about the shootings Merrillee broke into shards, like a pottery vase falling from the table. Mascara ran down her fat cheeks and the flesh on her arms shook like frozen sheets on a clothesline. When he came home, married to the black girl, Merrillee locked herself in her room and cried for a week, Mister Maestro wrote him out of the will and Zee, inexplicably, took all the blame onto herself, as if laughing that day he pulled his pants down had made all the difference. Thorne, who had hardly known him before, went secretly to see the couple, taking the train into New York by herself and riding the subway down to the east village. One time, she couldn't get out of her seat on the IRT and the police telephoned from the hospital.

There was a fire at the siding factory and Mister Maestro and Syd built a bigger one with the insurance money. Syd semi-retired and moved to Miami, from where he telephoned every Friday, just after six. There was no society for Parkinson's disease in Manasqua Park but Merrillee and Zee raised money for the Tuberculosis Association. In the studio in the rear of the siding factory, Mister Maestro continued his interest in photography, having advanced to color film. The girls who worked on the assembly line were always willing to do favors, and if they became too demanding, he got rid of them. There was no union.

"You know," Syd's voice said over the long distance wire, "there are great possibilities here. You should come down."

"I come every winter for three weeks."

"I don't mean for vacation. I mean to live. I was checking some land in the north, in some swamps or something, it's dirt cheap.

We could build a factory here and labor is half of what we pay up there."

"I thought it was hot there. What do they need aluminum siding for?"

"Listen, Mister, who ever said you were supposed to make business decisions? That's my job, no?"

"Merrillee wouldn't want to leave her friends. And Thorne has her specialist."

"So?"

"What do you mean, so? What, so?"

"So there's a law the whole family has to come?"

"You want Zee to disown me after all this time I invested?" They both laughed at that, Syd's froggy croak crackling over the long distance wire. Mister Maestro could picture Syd's adam's apple emerging from the swamp of fat to jiggle with laughter.

People who knew them said that Thorne's death had a great effect on Mister Maestro, but that was only true indirectly, since his love affair with the girl had long since cooled. The girl, who was eighteen and homely, had been making progress, the specialist said, taking her medicine faithfully and learning to keep the fits under control. The time between seizures became longer and longer. She and Merrillee were on their way to the specialist's midtown office, walking along Fifth Avenue, when a black man standing in the doorway of a boutique suddenly stepped into their path and punched her in the stomach.

Merrillee screamed and Thorne doubled over, vomiting blood.

"You bastard," Merrillee screamed at the black man, who strolled away in the midday sun, "her brother is married to one of your own people." But despite that invocation of his name, Tush wasn't notified and he didn't come to the funeral.

The lights went out of Zee's eyes and after the funeral she took to her room and rarely left it, except for meals. It was a lovely room, with new walnut furniture and a brocade spread on the double bed, which she had to share with no one. All her life, Zee had been cramped, jammed into an apartment built for sardines. Now she had a room of her own. There were pictures of Tush and Thorne at different ages stuck into the mirror frame. From her window, she could see a playground where children whose names she didn't know played. She was too strong to die right away but the following winter she went, leaving nothing in her will but the clothing Mister Maestro had bought for her to a poor cousin, and an Israel bond for $1,000 to Tush and his wife. At the funeral, her brother, Morris, took Mister Maestro aside and tapped him on the arm with a finger that had been cut off at the first joint by the butcher's knife with which he earned his living. "The whole family is grateful to you," Morris said, wiping real tears from his eyes. "You made poor Zee's life happy in her last years."

Mister Maestro waved his hand in a self-deprecating gesture, waiting for more. He and Uncle Morris had never been close.

"She had some life, Zee," Morris said. "That husband of hers, I don't have to tell you."

"No," Mister Maestro said.

"And that father of hers?" Uncle Morris tittered with embarrassment. "My father, too."

"Yes."

"Well, Meister, listen, if there's ever anything I or Charlotte can do for you, you let us know. You have the number, now keep in touch." In all the years they had known each other, Morris still thought Mister Maestro's first name was Meister, and Mister Maestro had never bothered to correct him.

"I'll do that, Uncle Morris," he said. "Have you met my associate, Sydney Lumut? Syd, come over here. Very nice of you, Uncle Morris."

"Not at all, Meister," Uncle Morris said. "You deserve it."

The house in Manasqua Park seemed very empty with only two of the five bedrooms in use. Without Zee to accompany her and Thorne for inspiration, Merrillee dropped her charitable work on behalf of the Tuberculosis Association. She said she would take up gardening instead, but she didn't. Mister Maestro, for his part, kept up the routine that had become the natural rhythm of his life in recent years: a few hours every day, rain or shine, at the factory, going over the books, if necessary, though it rarely was, since Syd, even from the distance of Miami, kept on top of things, but more often kidding with the girls on the floor; a few hours every day, in season, at Aquaduct or Monmouth Park race tracks; a few hours every week, regardless of what, in the studio at the rear of the factory. Then, suddenly, word came that Syd had choked on a mouthful of whitefish and died, and the phone ceased ringing on Friday evenings. Mister Maestro found himself spending more and more time at the factory, until last month, when there was a fire that almost destroyed the building. Something apparently went wrong and the police came the next day to talk about it. And the day after that, Mister Maestro came home early in the afternoon and found Merrillee watching television, an activity which had occupied her steadily for many months. On the day of Zee's funeral, she'd managed to get home in time for *Search for Tomorrow*.

"I want a divorce," Mister Maestro said in a flat, emotionless voice.

Merrillee didn't look up for a minute, until the commercial came on, and when she did, her eyes seemed to have trouble focusing on him. He stood silently, motionlessly waiting while she stared at him, adjusting the contrast with her eyes. "I want the house," she said abruptly.

Mister Maestro laughed. "That's the one thing you can't have. I sold the house. You can have the car."

She looked at him, stunned. The house was the only thing left she loved. "You bastard, you can't do that."

"Do it? I did it. This morning."

"I'll sue you, you pervert. I'll get it back."

It disturbed him that she should call him that but he laughed to show it didn't hurt. "Sue me, fine. That's what the courts are for. Maybe your son could use the business."

"Sue? That will just be the soup, you goddamn penguin. For the chopped liver, it'll be a call to the arson squad. For the gefilte fish, the morality squad. You think I'm going to take this lying down like your girls, you're crazy." Merrillee seemed stunned by her outburst and she turned her back on him, pacing across the room like a restless cat. She could feel blood surging through veins she thought had closed down.

"You can save yourself the trouble of the first call," Mister Maestro said lamely. He was surprised she knew about either that or the film-making and he stood uncertainly in the semi-darkness for a moment more before going upstairs to pack his suitcase.

"You won't get away with this, Mister," she yelled up the stairs. "This house is mine. I paid blood for it. You think my mother paid, that was nothing. You can't do this, I'll see you in jail, I'll see you dead."

Mister Maestro went to the bedroom door. "You think dead wouldn't be better than this?" he shouted back.

"You'll wish you *were* dead," Merrillee screamed. "You won't get a divorce, that's one thing for sure. You won't just brush me off like that. I'll never give you a divorce."

"Give, give, don't talk to me about give. I'll *take*, you goddamn slut."

"Ah, slut. Here it comes out. Slut? Slut? I should be so lucky. That's how you're going to do it? You think any judge with eyes in his head will look at me and believe I committed adultery? I should be so lucky." She began to laugh, her head thrown back, her voice rising like the wail of a fire siren. Mister Maestro walked down the stairs with his suitcase in his left hand, the fingers of his right nervously tugging at the smooth silk cuff above it. She wasn't in the hallway and the sound of the television set had been raised.

He called his lawyer from the hotel at the airport, listened intently and hung up. Syd had made the decisions for so long, it was hard to get his head to work the way he wanted it to, the way it had in the army and in Cleveland, even in Coney Island, in the early days. He stared at the receiver, nodding his head, then he called the New Jersey operator and asked for a number.

A young woman answered the phone.

"Uncle Morris?" Mister Maestro said tentatively.

There was a brief silence, then the young woman said, "No, this is his daughter, Bernice. Can I help you?"

"Bernice? This is Mister Maestro, your cousin, Zee's son-in-law?"

"Yes, Mister, how are you?"

"I'm very good, Bernice, very good. And you, you're well, I hope."

"Yes, I'm well."

"And your husband? And children? All well, I hope."

"Yes," Bernice said impatiently. If you listened carefully, it was clear the voice wasn't that of a young woman after all.

"Is, ah, Uncle Morris there?"

"No." A silence. "Was there anything I could help you with?"

"I wanted to talk to Uncle Morris," Mister Maestro said doggedly.

"My father died," Bernice said. "Several weeks ago. You're lucky to have caught us, we only came today to clean out the closets."

"I'm very sorry," Mister Maestro said. "He was a good man, Uncle Morris. A very good man. I'm only sorry I didn't know, the funeral...." His voice trailed off. "And, and your mother?" He thought for a moment. "Charlotte?"

"She's in a nursing home," Bernice said. She sounded tired, far away, like New Jersey was Florida or Ohio, someplace really distant.

"Ah," Mister Maestro said. He paused, thinking. "Listen, you can do me a favor."

"A favor? I....I'll try."

"What I was calling Uncle Morris about. He said, he told me he'd like to do me a good turn. It was a debt, actually. I did something for him, and he said he wanted to pay me back...."

"What is it?" Bernice interrupted. "What is it you want, Mister?"

"It's just a small thing. Something bigger, I wouldn't ask, believe me. Your cousin Merrillee and I, you know, Myrna, Myrna and I, we....we don't see eye to eye anymore, and we're....we're getting a divorce. I just need to be able to say I lived with your father, with Uncle Morris, for six months."

There was a long silence on the other end of the phone and Mister Maestro tugged at his cuffs, sweat running down his cheekbones. "My father was in a hospital for six months, Mister," Bernice said finally. "He had cancer. He was dying. He was having cobalt treatment and his hair fell out. He cried out in pain and sometimes there was nobody there to go to him."

"I didn't know," Mister Maestro said. "I would have been happy to visit him."

"You're crazy, Mister," Bernice said with sudden heat. "When we were children, we always made fun of you. I wanted you to know that."

"It was a debt....." Mister Maestro began to say, but she had hung up.

He took a cab to Coney Island and went for a walk. The building on Rockaway Avenue where they'd lived was gone, as was the photography studio on the corner, where a haberdashery had once been, and the hat factory, further down the street. There was a housing project there now, covering the whole neighborhood like a pile of dirty laundry. Little black children played in a courtyard and Mister Maestro stood watching them until a fat woman came out of a door and approached him menacingly.

He walked to the pier and stood out over the water, looking into the waves, imagining he could see the fish below, wiggling their tails in the cold. Their mouths opened silently, their sunken cheeks working effortlessly, their eyes staring. Once, years before, he had photographed a fish throught the clear glass walls of the aquarium, not far away. He had stood behind his own arrangement of glass, studying the motionless fish which stared back at him as he adjusted the focus, and thought how similar they were, he and the fish, their eyes popping, their mouths open. But the fish, of course, was free to swim away, that was the difference.

Mister Maestro put one leg over the railing and gazed deeper into the dark waves lapping noisily against the concrete pilings. He was about to slide his other leg over when he became conscious of eyes on him and turned his head to see a small black girl, one of the children from the project, gazing at him with wonder.

"What are you doing?" the girl asked timidly when she saw herself discovered. She had huge, luminous eyes and Mister Maestro found himself thinking of his camera again, thinking of the wonderful portrait she would make.

"I'm going to jump in," he said mildly. "Into the water."

"Can I watch?" the girl asked with a trace of excitement. She came closer to the railing but adjusted her feet to make sure she remained just out of Mister Maestro's reach.

He smiled. To his surprise, he was thinking of Thorne and Tush, and of Tush's wife, who might have looked like this girl when she was her age, and of their child, who might look like her now. His own children, he thought, had always been wrapped up in themselves, had never come close enough to him to watch or even to want to. Neither of them, not even Thorne when she was a child, had ever expressed interest in his cameras. "Sure, you can watch," he said, "but don't get yourself wet or your mother will be angry."

"You'll be able to float," the girl observed, pointing to Mister Maestro's hips, which, even beneath his suit, made him look like a bather wearing an inner tube. "Like a penguin."

Tears burned his eyes and he pulled himself erect on the other side of the railing. His hands were behind him, on the cold pipe, like the manacled hands of a prisoner. His fingers gave a final tug to his cuffs.

"What's your name?" the girl asked just before he loosened his grip.

He had to think for a moment before he answered: "Lemuel."